Roped In

A Blacktop Cowboys® Novella

By Lorelei James

1001 Dark Nights

EVIL EYE
CONCEPTS

Roped In
A Blacktop Cowboys® Novella
By Lorelei James

1001 Dark Nights
Copyright 2014 LJLA, LLC
ISBN: 978-1-940887-17-3

Forward: Copyright 2014 M. J. Rose
Published by Evil Eye Concepts, Incorporated

Sign up for the 1001 Dark Nights Newsletter
and be entered to win a Tiffany Key necklace.

There's a contest every month!

Go to http://www.1001darknights.com to subscribe.

As a bonus, all subscribers will receive a free
1001 Dark Nights story on 1/1/15.
The First Night
by Shayla Black, Lexi Blake & M.J. Rose

One Thousand and One Dark Nights

Once upon a time, in the future…

*I was a student fascinated with stories and learning.
I studied philosophy, poetry, history, the occult, and
the art and science of love and magic. I had a vast
library at my father's home and collected thousands
of volumes of fantastic tales.*

*I learned all about ancient races and bygone
times. About myths and legends and dreams of all
people through the millennium. And the more I read
the stronger my imagination grew until I discovered
that I was able to travel into the stories… to actually
become part of them.*

*I wish I could say that I listened to my teacher
and respected my gift, as I ought to have. If I had, I
would not be telling you this tale now.
But I was foolhardy and confused, showing off
with bravery.*

*One afternoon, curious about the myth of the
Arabian Nights, I traveled back to ancient Persia to
see for myself if it was true that every day Shahryar
(Persian: شهريار, "king") married a new virgin, and then
sent yesterday's wife to be beheaded. It was written
and I had read, that by the time he met Scheherazade,
the vizier's daughter, he'd killed one thousand
women.*

Something went wrong with my efforts. I arrived in the midst of the story and somehow exchanged places with Scheherazade — a phenomena that had never occurred before and that still to this day, I cannot explain.

Now I am trapped in that ancient past. I have taken on Scheherazade's life and the only way I can protect myself and stay alive is to do what she did to protect herself and stay alive.

Every night the King calls for me and listens as I spin tales. And when the evening ends and dawn breaks, I stop at a point that leaves him breathless and yearning for more. And so the King spares my life for one more day, so that he might hear the rest of my dark tale.

As soon as I finish a story... I begin a new one... like the one that you, dear reader, have before you now.

Prologue

Steer wrestler Sutton Grant knew the instant he threw himself off his horse he was in for a world of hurt.

He'd miscalculated the distance and his rate of rotation. The last thing he remembered before he hit the steer was he could kiss this year's world championship title good-bye.

He woke up in the ambulance, his head pounding, unable to move any part of his body but his eyes.

Fuck.

Try and move.

I can't.

Was he paralyzed?

He couldn't be.

What if he was? He'd never hurt like this. Never.

But the fact he could feel pain had to be good, right?

Maybe the intense pain is your body shutting down.

If he was paralyzed, who would shoulder the burden of caring for him for the rest of his life? He didn't have a wife or a girlfriend. Would responsibility fall to his family?

Oh, hell no. He'd put them through enough with his last rodeo mishap.

Mishap? Don't you mean accident that kept you out of commission for a year? Do you remember living at home and seeing the worry on your parent's faces?

That'd been worse than the months of physical and mental recovery. Then he'd had the added burden of seeing their happiness vanish after he'd healed and had informed them he planned to return to the sport.

His mother's voice drifted into his memory. *You're still going to do this even if it hurts, maims, or kills you?* He'd responded, *Even then.*

He still saw the tear tracks on her face, the subtle shake of her head. And he'd still gone off anyway, chasing the gold buckle, putting his body through hell.

I take it back! I didn't mean it!

Right then and there, Sutton made a bargain with God:

Please Lord, if I survive this with my body intact, I swear I'll give up bulldoggin' forever. No lie. I'll be done for good.

White lights blinded him and for a brief instant, he thought he'd died. A voice he'd never heard before whispered to him, *promise accepted.*

Then darkness descended again. The last thing Sutton remembered was wiggling his fingers and toes and whispering a prayer of thanks.

Chapter One

Eight months later...

"You ain't supposed to be out there doin' that," Wynton shouted.

Sutton looked across the paddock at his older brother and scowled. He tugged on the reins but his horse Dial wouldn't budge. Damn stubborn horse; he had to be part mule.

"I've got a ridin' crop you can borrow," his younger brother Creston yelled from atop the corral fence.

"I'm surrounded by smartasses," Sutton informed Dial. "And apparently I'm a dumbass because I never learn with you, do I?"

Dial tossed his mane.

After he climbed off his horse, Sutton switched out the bit and bridle for a lead rope. Then he opened the gate between the paddock and the pasture, playfully patting Dial's flank as the gray dun tore off.

Dial actually kicked up his hooves in glee as he galloped away.

"Yeah, I'll miss our special time together too, asshole."

Asshole. Man, he was punchier than he realized if he was calling his horse an asshole.

Sutton sauntered over to where his brothers waited for him, surprised that they'd both shown up in the middle of a Friday afternoon—with a six-pack. Wyn and Cres both ranched with their dad, although as the oldest, Wyn had inherited the bulk of the ranch work decisions. It appeared he'd changed the rule about working a full day—every day, rain, shine, snow, come hell, high water, or wild fire.

"What's the occasion? You here to borrow money?" he asked.

"Good one. Glad to see they didn't remove all of your funny bone after surgery," Wyn said dryly.

"Hilarious." Sutton quirked an eyebrow at Cres. "Got something smart to say?"

"Yeah. You know you ain't supposed to be doin' anything that'll further injure you. When we hadn't heard from you all week, we figured you were up to no good. And I see we were right."

"It wasn't like I was bulldoggin'."

"This'd be a different conversation if we'd seen you doin' that." Wyn handed him a beer. "We ain't trying to bust your balls, but goddammit, Sutton. You almost fucking died."

"*Again*," Cres added.

"Well, I ain't dead. But don't feel like I'm alive, either." He sipped the cold brew. Nothing tasted better on a hot summer day.

"Should we be on suicide watch?" Wyn said hesitantly.

Sutton had a mental break the last time he'd been injured, so his family kept an eye on him, and he knew how lucky he was to have that support. "Nah. It's just this sitting around, healing up stuff is driving me bugshit crazy."

"The way to deal with your boredom ain't to get in the cage with your demon and go another round."

Sutton squinted at Cres. "You callin' my horse a demon?"

Cres rolled his eyes. "No, dipshit. Your demon is the need to prove yourself. Regardless of the cost."

His gaze met his youngest brother's. Growing up, Wyn and Cres joked about Sutton being the mailman's kid because he was the only one of the three boys with blue-green eyes. Both his brothers and his parents had brown eyes. Sometimes he wondered if that outsider status is what lured him into the world of professional rodeo and away from working on the family ranch.

He sighed. "I appreciate your concern, I really do. I'm just frustrated. Makes it worse when I hafta deal with Dial. He's a temperamental motherfucker on his best days. I don't trust anyone to work with him after that last go around with the so-called 'expert,' which means he ain't getting the proper workout for a horse of his caliber."

"A few months cooling his hooves shouldn't have changed his previous training that much. Breeders take mares out of bucking contention, as well as barrel racing, when they're bred. Sometimes that'd be up to two years."

"I know that. But Dial? He ain't like other horses. Gelding him didn't dampen that fire; if anything, it increased his orneriness."

"I'd be ornery too if some dude sliced off my balls," Wyn said with a shudder. Then he looked at Sutton. "So that other bulldogger, the guy with the weird name...what happened the weekend he borrowed him?"

"Weird name." Sutton snorted. "That's rich coming from a guy named *Wynton*."

"Fuck off, *Sutton*," he shot back. "I think Mom was high on child birthin' painkillers when she picked our names."

"Probably. You talkin' about Breck Christianson? He tried to help me out during the Western Livestock Show in January while I was still laid up."

"Yeah. Him." Wyn looked at Cres. "Don't know if I ever heard you talk about what went down that week you were there with him and Dial."

Cres rested his forearms on the top of the fence and his hat shadowed his face. "It was a damn disaster in the arena. Dial wouldn't do nothin'. Seriously. That high-strung bastard stayed in the damn chute. The one time he left the chute, he charged the hazer's horse. Breck traveled to Denver specifically to get a feel for Dial before the competition, but he ended up sticking with his own mount."

"Huh. Surprised you stayed in Denver for the whole stock show since it meant you had to take care of demon horse while you were there."

Cres shrugged. "I never get to see the behind the chutes action for a week-long event. It was interesting and everyone was friendly."

"So Breck took good care of you?" Sutton asked.

Cres choked on his beer.

Wyn patted him on the back. "You okay?"

"Yeah." *Cough cough.* "A bug flew in my mouth." Another cough. "Breck introduced me around."

Sutton nudged his shoulder. "Breck introduce you to his buckle bunny pussy posse?"

Before Cres responded, Wyn interrupted. "Cres wouldn't know what to do with the ladies. The kid is all work and no play. He probably spent all his time hidin' in the horse trailer."

"I ain't a kid," Cress said tightly. "And don't assume you know what I got up to because you don't. Anyway, Breck knows everyone." He looked at Sutton. "He introduced me to Saxton Green, that other bulldogger you get mistaken for all the time. He's built like you, even looks like you, but he sure don't act like you. That man is fuckin' wild."

Sutton groaned. "Do you know how many times I've had to defend myself against something Saxton did? It sucks. That's about the only time I don't mind that the other competitors call me 'The Saint.'"

"Other competitors, and everyone else involved with the rodeo circuit, including the women, call you 'The Saint' because you're the one who acts like a freakin' monk," Wyn pointed out helpfully. "Damn man. How do you turn down all that free pussy?"

"It ain't free, trust me," Sutton retorted.

"Wyn, leave him alone," Cres said. "Stop acting like you've got it rough and ain't getting your fair share of tail. Women are lined up in your driveway to get a piece of you."

Wyn smirked and raised his beer. "It's good to be me."

Cres rolled his eyes. "Oh, and I also met the couple who raised and trained Dial before you bought him."

That piqued Sutton's interest. "Chuck and Berlin Gradsky? Really?"

"They were in the arena when Breck was having a hard time with Dial. Neither of them even tried to step in. They said the only people who had any effect on him was you and their daughter who'd trained him."

London Gradsky. He hadn't thought of her in a couple of years. The surly brunette who'd thrown a shit fit when her parents had sold Dial to him rather than just continuing to let him compete on the horse. She'd accused him of taking advantage of her parents, caring about his career above the welfare of the animal. Then she'd launched into a diatribe about how self-absorbed he was for pushing to have the stallion castrated without considering the long-term gains for breeding. After calling him a dickhead whose belt buckle was bigger than his brain, she'd stormed off.

Chuck and Berlin explained away her behavior, fondly referring to her as their headstrong filly. They were proud that she'd struck out on her own as a horse trainer rather than just expecting to get a primo position at Grade A Horse Farms because her parents owned the business. But still, London's accusations had stung. What he wouldn't give for her expertise now. Although it'd been three years since their altercation, he doubted the feisty firecracker would let bygones be bygones. "Well, it's obvious I need help."

"What about that Eli guy?" Wyn said. "Didn't you say he's some kind of Native American horse whisperer?"

"Eli is top notch. But Dial's temperament is particularly bad around other horses. He took a chunk outta the alpha horse the one time I left him there—this was after Eli put him in a pasture by himself and he jumped the fence. So Dial is no longer welcome."

"I have faith you'll figure something out that doesn't entail you bein' on the dirt with him."

Cres straightened up and moved to toss his bottle into the shooting barrel. "To be blunt, as much as we care for our animals, bro, they are tools. Tools are replaceable. You are not. This last time you nearly went into kidney failure, liver failure, and they talked of removing your spleen. Both me'n Wyn would've offered up a kidney or even a damn lung for you. You know that. We'd rather not have to face that choice again."

"We're askin' you not to do something that'll put you back in the hospital for another six weeks followed by months of recovery." Wyn gestured to the ranch house and the area around them. "You've got a nice place to hang your hat, money in the bank, the kinda looks that get any woman you want into your bed, and family nearby. Ain't nothin' wrong with that life."

Sutton watched his brothers drive off. He put the three bottles left from the six-pack into the fridge in the garage, knowing he'd be less tempted to drink them all if he had to leave the house to get them.

He changed clothes, flipped on the ball game for some background noise, and snagged his laptop. He typed London Gradsky in the search engine. The top result read:

London's Bridge To Training A Better Horse

Seriously? That was the worst fucking business slogan he'd ever heard. He clicked on the link.

Hers was a simple website. Contact info via e-mail or phone. Testimonials about her training successes. Links to horse brokers and breeders—no surprise Grade A Horse Farms topped the list—but nowhere did London list her lineage. Interesting.

Lastly, he saw a page with a schedule of summer events.

Sutton scrolled the page. Evidently, London put on training clinics on the weekends during the summer at local fairs and rodeos. For fifty bucks, she'd spend thirty minutes assessing the horse and rider before offering training recommendations.

The cynical side of his brain remembered her cutting words to him and weighed in with: *What are the odds she recommends herself as the horse trainer who can miraculously fix bad habits and riders?*

But his optimist side crawled out of the dark hole it'd been hiding in since the accident and countered with: *Her business wouldn't last long if she didn't get results, and the horse training world in Colorado would shun her if she was a shyster.*

It looked to him like she'd been putting on these summer clinics for at least a couple years. And every time slot was booked, as well as several people on standby for an open appointment. He scrolled down to the current week's schedule and his heart skipped a beat.

Score.

She'd be in Fairfax, Colorado, this weekend. That was only thirty miles from here. And score again. Her last slot of the day was still open.

With zero hesitation, he typed in D.L. A-ride and hoped liked hell she had a sense of humor.

And that she wouldn't chase after him with a horse whip when she realized who he was.

Chapter Two

Worst. Morning. Ever.

London Gradsky glared at the busted coffee maker. She'd spent twenty minutes fiddle-fucking around with the thing to try and get it to work. Giving it up as a lost cause, she'd chucked the whole works outside.

No coffee in her cozy camper meant she had to go to the exhibitors' and contestants' tent to get her morning jolt of caffeine. Since she'd just planned on quickly ducking in and out, she hadn't combed her hair, washed her face, brushed her teeth, or changed out of her pajamas.

And motherfucking, son of a bitch if *they* weren't there, Tweedledee and Tweedletwat. Making cowpie eyes at each other while people looked at them with indulgent smiles. She could almost hear the collective sigh of the women in the tent when Stitch gently wiped a smear of powdered sugar off Paige's cheek then kissed the spot.

Paige giggled and nuzzled him. Her tiara caught on the brim of his cowboy hat, which sent the newly anointed golden couple's admirers scurrying forward to help them out of such a huge pickle.

Of course no one pointed out how stupid it was that Paige actually *wore* a fucking tiara to breakfast. The man-stealing bitch probably wore it to bed. Then London drifted into a fantasy where Paige had donned the tiara when she gave Stitch a blowjob and it cut the hell out of his abdomen.

"Sending eye daggers at her while eye fucking him ain't smart, London," her on-the-road partner in crime Melissa "Mel" Lockhart said behind her.

"I'm not eye fucking him, I'm eye fucking him *up*."

"Doesn't matter, because that's not how anyone will see it. Come on, let's get out of here."

London allowed herself to be led away. As soon as they were out of screeching range, she exploded. "How in the fuck am I gonna survive this summer, Mel? When every time I turn around I see them sucking each other's faces off? What does he see in her?"

Mel didn't answer. She appeared to be hedging, which was not her usual style.

"Just spit it out."

"Fine. That girl is a bonafide beauty queen. Everyone says she'll be the next Miss Rodeo America and people treat him like he's a prince—the heir apparent to take that All Around title at the CRA Championships in a few years. They are a match made in PR heaven. What don't you get about that?"

"I don't get how that asswipe could dump me, via text message, after he does one fundraiser with her because it's true love? Bullshit. No one falls in love in a night." London paced along the metal fencing. "I wanna choke her with her stupid 'Miss Rodeo Colorado' sash and then tie it around his dick until it turns blue and falls off."

Mel's hands landed on London's shoulders and then she was right in her face, her brown eyes flashing concern. "This has gotta stop, London. What the hell did you see in him anyway? He's looks like Opie from *The Andy Griffith Show*. I think the only reason you ended up with him in the first place is because you were lonely and wanted a dog."

"He's a damn hound dog who needs to be put down," she muttered.

"Not true, because we both know that man did not rock your world or even the damn camper when you two got down and dirty. He doesn't know how to be a horndog."

London couldn't argue that point.

"Seriously sista, you're starting to scare me with all these violent scenarios you spout off like horror poetry. Stitch scratching an itch with Paige the underage is not the end of the world. I think the real issue here is you need to get laid by a man who knows what he's doing. And you're putting out this I-will-rip-your-dick-off vibe to any man who starts sniffing around you."

That wasn't true…was it?

"Find a hot guy and fuck him 'til he can't walk. Then you'll be back to strutting around with your head held high instead of acting like a whipped pup."

"You're right."

"Of course I am. Now take a minute and breathe."

London closed her eyes, inhaled for ten counts, exhaled for ten, and reopened her eyes to gaze at her friend.

The freckle-faced redhead wore a smug look. "Better?"

"Much. Thank you." Then her gaze narrowed. "Hey, you just did that thing my mother always does. Did she give you instructions on how to get me to cool off?"

"Yes, and I asked her—but she didn't offer up her magic mom trick freely."

"When were you hanging out with my mother?" London demanded.

"Uh, since she *owns* my cutting horse, I see her more than you do."

"She may own your horse, but I trained Plato so he'll always love me best."

"Even my color blind horse can see what you're wearing is all kinds of wrong because you look like a leprechaun hag. Where *did* you get those god-awful green pajamas?" Mel leaned closer. "Do they have frogs on them? And sweet baby Jesus on a Vespa...are those frogs baring lipstick-kissed butt cheeks?"

"Yep. Nana gave them to me after Stitch ditched me. Said toads like him could kiss my ass."

"Appropriate I guess, but still hideous. Come to my horse trailer. I've got coffee and everything to banish that outer hag." She smirked. "You're on your own getting rid of that inner hag."

"Fuck off."

"You love me."

"I really do." She looped her arm through Mel's. "Let's start making a 'get London laid' list of candidates." She paused. "You still got your little black book of rodeo circuit bad boys?"

"Yep. It's even color coded by cock size, which circuit they're on, and their ability to last longer than eight seconds."

* * * *

London was hot and tired, but exhilarated after six hours of working with horses and their riders. About three quarters of her clientele were kids under fourteen. It was gratifying, proving to novice equestrians that their animal was under their control. Contrary to belief, she picked up very few new regular clients at fairs and rodeos. The problems she helped with were rider related rather than horse related. The horse issues would take more than a thirty minute fix.

She checked her sign-up list, surprised to see her last opening had been filled. Weird name. D.L. A-ride. No gender or age listed. Was it a joke? D.L. A-ride. She watched the gate for a horse and rider to approach.

After two minutes she closed her eyes, breathing in the familiar scents of hot dirt and manure and livestock, with the occasional whiff of diesel fuel and something sugary like cotton candy or funnel cakes or Bavarian almonds.

"Excuse me," a deep voice said behind her. "I'm looking for London Gradsky?"

London pushed off the fence and turned around, but the *you found her* response dried on her tongue. Holy balls was this man hot. Like off the charts hot. Two days' worth of dark scruff couldn't hide the sharp angles of his face. Strong, almost square jaw, ridiculously full lips. The guy wore a ball cap and dark shades. A short-sleeved polo in ocean blue accentuated the breadth of his shoulders, the contours of his chest and... Holy smoking double barrels, welcome to the gun show; his biceps were huge. His forearms appeared to have been carved out of marble. She stopped herself from dropping her gaze to his crotch. Had Mel sent this man her way?

"I'm London. Do I know you?" *Please don't tell me you're a long lost cousin or something.*

"Yeah. We met a while back." He paused. "I signed up for the last class slot because I needed to talk to you."

Needed. Not wanted. Her skepticism reared its snappish head. "Who are you?"

He encroached on her space, completely throwing her body into shadow and tumult. Then she waited, breath trapped in her lungs for the moment when he tore off his sunglasses.

Eyes as blue as the Caribbean stared back at her.

Fuck me. She knew those eyes. She'd dreamt of those eyes. Although last time she'd seen them up close she'd wanted to spit in them. "Sutton Grant."

"I reckon a once-over like that is better than the fiery look of hatred I expected." He grinned.

That grin? With the damn dimples in his cheeks and in his chin? Not fair. She was *such* a sucker for a devil's smile boosted by pearly whites. But she'd considered him devil's spawn after his dealings with her family. In her mind she'd attributed cloven hooves, demon horns, and a forked tongue and tail to him.

Which pissed her off because the man was a piece of art. A real piece of work, too, if he thought she'd let bygones be bygones just so she could stare slack-jawed at his perfect face, spellbinding eyes, and banging body.

"You lied to get a meeting with me?" She snorted. "I see you're still the same manipulative bastard who follows his own agenda."

He took another step closer. "I see you're still the same brat who jumps to conclusions."

"Yeah? I'm not the one in a piss-poor disguise, douche-nozzle."

"Douche-nozzle...I don't even know what that is."

"Look in the mirror, pal." Her gaze flicked over him. "A ball cap, a polo shirt, and...no freakin' way. Are you wearing *Mom* jeans, Sutton Grant?"

He shot a quick look around and said, "Keep your voice down. No one has recognized me and I'd like to keep it that way."

"I'll bet your girlfriend picked this outfit because it is guaranteed to keep you from getting laid. Like ever."

He scowled. "I don't have a girlfriend. Now can we skip the insults and cut to the chase? Because I really need to talk to you."

"You scheduled the time and it ain't free." London held out her hand. "Fifty bucks for thirty minutes. The clock starts ticking as soon as you pay up."

Sutton dug in his front pocket and pulled out a crumpled fifty. "Here."

"Shoot."

"It's about Dial."

"What did you do to him?"

"It's more a problem of what I'm *not* doin' with him. Due to my injury, he's been benched the last eight months."

Now she remembered. Sutton had gotten badly hurt late last fall during his circuit's last qualifying event for the CRA Finals and ended up with life-threatening internal injuries. "What do you want from me?"

"I'll hire you to work with Dial, get him back up to speed, since I'm still sidelined."

"So he'll be in top condition when you're back on the circuit?"

A funny look flitted through his eyes and he looked away. "Something like that."

"Why me?"

"Because we both know the only people who've been able to work with him have been you and me."

She sucked in a few breaths and forced herself to loosen her fists. "This wouldn't be an issue if you hadn't browbeaten my folks into selling Dial to you outright. When the breeder owns the horse and a rider goes down, other people are in place to keep the horse conditioned. That responsibility isn't pushed aside."

"You think I don't know that? You think I'm feelin' good about any of this? Fuck. I hired people to work with him and the stubborn bastard chased them all off. A couple of them literally."

London smirked. "That's my boy."

"Your boy is getting fatter and meaner by the day," Sutton retorted. "I'm afraid if I let him go too much longer it'll be too late and he'll be as worthless as me."

Worthless? Dude. Look in the mirror much? How could Sutton be out of commission and still look like he'd stepped off the pages of *Buff and Beautiful Bulldogger* magazine?

"I hope the reason you're so quiet is because you're considering my offer."

London's gaze zoomed to his. "How do you know you can afford me?"

"I don't. I get that you're an expert on this particular horse and I'm willing to pay you for that expertise." Sutton sidestepped her and rested his big body next to hers—close to hers—against the fence. "I know it'll sound stupid, but every time I grab the tack and head out to catch Dial to try and work him, even when I'm not supposed to, I feel his frustration that I'm not doin' more. I ain't the kind of man that sees a horse—my horse—as just a tool. Your folks knew that about me or they wouldn't have sold him to me for any amount of money."

"Yeah. I do know that," she grudgingly admitted, "but you should also know that I wouldn't be doin' this for you or the money, I'd be doin' it for Dial."

"That works for me. There's another reason that I want you. Only you."

"Which is?"

His unwavering stare unnerved her, as if he was gauging whether he could trust her. Finally he said, "Strictly between us?"

She nodded.

"If it's decided I'll never compete again, you're in the horse world more than I am and you'll ensure Dial gets where he needs to be."

London hadn't been expecting that. Sutton had paid a shit ton for Dial, and he hadn't suggested she'd help him sell the horse to a proper owner, just that she'd help him find one. In her mind that meant he really had Dial's best interest at heart. Not that she believed for an instant Sutton Grant intended to retire from steer wrestling. First off, he was barely thirty. Second, rumor had it his drive to win was as wide and deep as the Colorado River.

As she contemplated how to respond, she saw her ex, Stitch, with Princess Paige plastered to his side, meandering their direction.

Dammit. Not now.

After the incident this morning, she'd steered clear of the exhibitor's hall where the pair had handed out autographs and barf bags. She felt the overwhelming need to escape, but if she booked it across the corral, it'd look like she was running from them.

Screw that. Screw them. She was not in the wrong.

"London? You look ready to commit murder. What'd I say?"

She gazed up at him. The man was too damn good-looking, so normally she wouldn't have a shot at a man like him. But he did say he'd do *anything*...

"Okay, here's the deal. I'll work with Dial, but you've gotta do something for me. Uh, two things actually."

"Name them."

How much to tell him? She didn't want to come off desperate. Still, she opted for the truth. "Backstory: my boyfriend dumped me via text last month because he'd hooked up with a rodeo queen. Because he and I were together when I made my summer schedule, that means I will see them every fucking weekend. All summer."

"And?"

"And I don't wanna be known as that poor pathetic London Gradsky pining over her lost love."

Sutton's eyes turned shrewd. "*Are* you pining for him?"

"Mostly I'm just pissed. It needs to look like I've moved on. So I realize your nickname is 'The Saint' and you don't—"

"Don't call me that," he said crossly. "Tell me what you need."

"The first thing I'd need is you to play the part of my new boyfriend."

That shocked him, but he rallied with, "I can do that. When does this start?"

"Right now, 'cause here they come." London plastered her front to his broad chest and wreathed her arms around his neck. "And make this look like the real deal, bulldogger."

"Any part of you that's hands off for me?"

She fought the urge to roll her eyes. Of course "The Saint" would ask first. "Nope."

Sutton bestowed that fuck-me-now grin. "I can work with that." He curled one hand around the back of her neck and the other around her hip.

When it appeared he intended to take his own sweet time kissing her, she took charge, teetering on tiptoe since the man was like seven feet tall. After the first touch of their lips, he didn't dive into her mouth in a fake show of passion. He rubbed his half-parted lips across hers, each pass silently coaxing her to open up a little more. Each tease of his breath on her damp lips made them tingle.

She muttered, "Kiss me like you mean business."

Those deceptively gentle kisses vanished and Sutton unleashed himself on her. Lust, passion, need. The kiss was way more powerful and take charge than she'd expected from a man nicknamed "The Saint."

Her mind shut down to everything but the sensuous feel of his tongue twining around hers as he explored her mouth, the soft stroking of his thumb on her cheek, and the possessive way his hand stroked her, as if it knew her intimately.

Then Sutton eased back, treating her lips to nibbles, licks, and lingering smooches. "Think they're gone?" he murmured.

"Who?"

He chuckled. "Your ex."

"Oh. Right. Them." She untwined her fingers from his soft hair and let her arms drop—slowly letting her hands flow over his neck and linebacker shoulders and that oh-so-amazing chest.

Their gazes collided the second she realized Sutton's heart beat just as crazily as hers did.

"So did that pass as the real deal kiss you wanted? Or do I need to do it again?"

Yes, please.

Don't be a pushover. Let him know who's in charge.

London smoothed her hand down her blouse. "For future reference, that type of kiss will work fine."

Sutton smirked. "It worked *fine* for me too, darlin'."

His face, his body, his voice—everything about him tripped her every trigger. The man would be hell on her libido.

Or you could be hell on his. Take Mel's advice. Getcha some mattress action. See exactly what it'd take to get "The Saint" all hot under the collar.

When she smiled at him, his body stiffened. "Why do you look so nervous?"

"Because that devious smile you're sporting is scary. So let's skip what it means for now. You said you needed two things from me before you'd agree to work with Dial. First is this boyfriend fake out stuff. What's the other?"

"I need a place to crash. Since I'll be working with your horse every day, I'll be crashing with you for the summer."

Chapter Three

Crashing with him?

What the bleeding hell?

He opened his mouth to protest and London laughed. "Dude, you oughta see the look on your face!"

"So you were just dicking with me?"

Her smile dried. "Sorta."

"Explain...sorta?"

"Okay. Fine. I've been living in my camper since Stitch ditched me."

"Stitch? Seriously? Your ex's name is Stitch? Is he really funny or something?"

London rolled her eyes. "No. His given name is Barclay or something stupidly stuffy. The year he turned five he was in the emergency room for stitches like ten times. The doctor said they oughta change his name to Stitch and it stuck. Anyway, I didn't have any place to go after his breakup text."

"Why didn't you go home? I've been to your house. It's huge." He paused. "Did you have a falling out with your parents?"

"No. But I'm twenty-seven. Returning home...I'd feel like a failure. I've been on my own for years. I only gave up my apartment because I was practically living at Stitch's anyway." She looked away. "I thought the relationship would be permanent. When it turned out not to be? I should've followed my mom's advice to always take care of myself first and to not give away things for free."

"Meaning...why buy the cow when you're giving the milk away for free?" he teased.

"No. Meaning I trained Stitch's horse. That's part of the reason he's done so good on the circuit this year."

His gut clenched. "He didn't pay you?"

She shook her head. "Worse. I didn't charge him." Absentmindedly, she traced the polo logo on his left pec and his nipple hardened. "I've been meaning to look for a place to live that's centrally located, but my summer schedule is busy and I don't seem to have enough time."

"But you'd have time to work with Dial?"

"Yes, especially if I'm onsite with him. I just need a place to park my camper. That's it. I won't bother you at all. My morning training appointments don't start until ten. I'm usually done by six in the evening." Her gaze hooked his. "Wait. You don't live at home, do you?"

"No. I have my own place. Why?"

"I just thought maybe your injuries were such that you moved home again so your family could help you out. I remember my mom mentioning—"

"The last time I injured myself in the arena was five years ago, and yes, *that* time I did return home. As soon as I dealt with some issues, I finished the house I'd started to build for my ex. After I'd changed the layout so it was what I wanted not what she'd demanded."

London's hazel eyes softened. "Glad to see I'm not the only one with baggage from an ex."

"You have no idea."

"Then tell me."

"Why?"

"If we're involved I'd know stuff like this. Plus, I'm nosy. So dish on the biggest bag."

Christ, she was pushy. "I met Charlotte when I started competing professionally in college. We were young. She knew what she wanted. I was too...green to see it."

"See what? That she just wanted you for your green?"

"Clever. She wanted a man who made a good living but was gone all the time. After my career setback and the injuries that required multiple surgeries...I was off the circuit. That meant no money coming in and I'd be underfoot expecting her to take care of me. She bailed on me the second week of my recovery."

"Harsh. That sucks."

Sutton let himself get a full look at this woman he'd spent a good five minutes kissing. High forehead and cheekbones. Dark eyebrows and eyelashes. Her eyes were more green than brown. With her auburn hair and fair complexion he expected to see freckles, but her skin was smooth. Flawless. Her lips, when they weren't flattened into an angry line, were pink and lush and way too tempting. If he had to describe her heart-shaped face with one word he'd say...sweet.

"Why the fuck are you gawking at me, bulldogger?"

And…not so sweet. Undeterred, he traced the curve of her neck, intrigued by how her pulse jumped at his touch. "Because it's one of the first times you've let me. And darlin', you *are* a pretty sight when you ain't scowling at me."

She blushed. But she didn't move away from his touch. "Can I ask you something?"

"Sure."

"Were you ever a player?"

"How would you react if I said yes?"

London considered him for a moment. "I'd be surprised."

"Why?"

"You seem more settled than the last time we crossed paths."

Wrong. He'd never been more unsettled, which was proof people saw what they wanted. "Not to disagree, but you were so busy painting me as the enemy back then that's all you saw. I'm not a bad guy; I was just trying to prove myself in the arena. Any of the player stuff I get accused of is because I get mixed up with Saxton Green."

She snorted. "I've met him. He doesn't hold a candle to you." London realized she'd paid him a compliment and backtracked. "Well, hate to burst your bubble, pal, but you'll still be proving yourself to me."

They realized, simultaneously, they were still body to body, face to face. But when London tried to bolt, Sutton wouldn't let her. "Steady. Don't want the people watching us to think we had a tiff after that kiss, would we?"

Her eyes widened. "Do you think there are people watching us?"

"I know there are, because darlin', that was some kiss."

Her lips curved into a smile. "Yes, it was."

Sutton pressed his lips to her forehead. "Let's head to your camper to finish this discussion in private before my thirty minutes are up."

London retreated, took his hand and said, "This way."

On the walk to where the competitors and exhibitors had set up camp, London said hello to several people but didn't introduce him, and luckily no one recognized him.

Her camper was the pull-behind kind—not fifth wheel sized, but the funky silver-bullet Airstream type. He noticed it was still hooked up to her truck. "When did you get here?"

"Late yesterday afternoon." She unlocked the camper door. "After you."

Sutton hadn't known what to expect when he'd stepped inside, so the vibrant color scheme filled in the blanks about what kind of person London was in the hours off the dirt.

Crafting stuff covered every inch of surface area across the small table. "I function in creative chaos and don't normally have visitors."

"What'd the smashed coffee pot on the ground outside do to get tossed out?"

"Quit working."

"Ah." He leaned against the wall while she packed things away. "You're lucky you've got this much space. Bad thing about bein' on the road is there's never enough room in the living quarters of a horse trailer."

"That's why my mom insisted I get this. She has no problem hauling horses, but she insists on sleeping in a hotel."

"Smart lady."

"So, Sutton, what do you do during the day at home since you aren't training or on the road?"

"Physical therapy some days," he lied. Those days were behind him. "Other days, I'm a great gate opener when my dad and brothers need extra help on the ranch."

London looked up sharply. "You don't ranch?"

He shook his head. "Growing up a rancher's kid, I never saw the appeal, just all the damn work."

"I hear ya there. I didn't date ranchers' kids because I never wanted to be a rancher's wife." She sorted beads and strips of twine into a plastic catch-all container with dozens of different compartments. "Does this feel awkward to you?" she asked without meeting his gaze.

"What? Me bein' in your camper?"

"That, and the fact that we'll be spending a lot of time together over the next few weeks. An hour ago, we were strangers who'd spoken just one time and now we've played a pretty intense round of tonsil hockey, and here we are alone."

He laughed. "If I think too hard on it, yeah, it'd seem weird. But I approached you, London. I figured that my offer would catch you off guard."

"As I'm sure my counter offer did you."

"Yeah. Well, I ain't exactly sure how that'll work."

London's shoulders stiffened.

"That came out wrong. What I meant is we're acting like a couple only on the weekends?"

"Saturdays are my workshops, so I'd like you to be around after my sessions end."

"Not before?"

"I don't expect world champion steer wrestler Sutton Grant to stand around holding my clipboard and collecting payments."

"You'd be surprised at what I'd do to get a sense of purpose these days," he said dryly.

She smiled and kept packing stuff away. "If the rodeo finals are held on

Sunday, there's usually a dance Saturday night. I'd like to put in an appearance because that'd be normal for me. And since we're together..." She glanced up at him. "Speaking of, what will we tell those nosy people who ask how we ended up falling in *lurve* so suddenly?"

Sutton scratched his chin. He really needed to shave. And make sure he didn't dress like a bum. No daily schedule meant he'd gotten lax on dressing the cowboy way, as he'd done for years. "How about the truth? I was havin' behavioral issues with Dial. I knew you'd trained him so I asked you for help. We spent a lot of time together and that's our *lurve* story."

"Perfect." She snapped the locks on her huge plastic tote. "Done."

"What is all that anyway?"

"Like I said, creative chaos. I'm the super high-energy type, which means I always need to be doing something. Making jewelry forces me to focus and slow down. It's a hobby, but since I'm so task oriented, I'm very prolific."

He could see that. "How many pieces you finish in a night?"

London shrugged. "At least two. Some nights as many as ten."

"Sweet Christ, woman. What do you do with them?"

"They're in plastic tubs in the bedroom. Hell, I think there might even be some tubs on the bed. Not like the bed has seen any action lately."

We could remedy that. Right now.

She seemed embarrassed by her confession. Before she fled, Sutton hooked a finger in her belt loop, stopping her.

"Whoa there. No running away. Especially not in here since there's no room for me to chase you, darlin'."

Her eyes blazed. "Let go."

"Nope. You're gonna tell me what you meant when you said the bed hadn't seen any action."

"That's none of your damn business."

"Wrong. Every low-down dirty personal detail about you is now my business bein's we're a couple in *lurve*." To reinforce his point, he crowded her against the cabinet. "If I remember correctly, you said your ex broke up with you a month ago. So it's been a month since that mattress has had a real pounding?"

"That mattress has been jostled and bounced, but it's *never* been pounded."

Sutton quirked an eyebrow. "Stitch too much of a gentleman to give you a good hard fuck?"

The fire in her eyes died. "Just drop it."

"How long's it been for you, London?"

"Four months."

"Motherfuckin' hell. What was wrong with that asswipe? He had sexy you in his bed and he left you alone for three goddamned months?"

"Yes. Apparently he was getting what he needed from Paige so he didn't touch me. I made excuses for his behavior. He was stressed, I was too pushy, I was too kinky. You name it, I took the blame." She sighed and studied the logo on his shirt again.

"No sirree. You ain't takin' the blame for him bein' a total douche-nozzle."

That brought a smile.

"And I will tell you something else."

"What?"

"I will take complete blame for this." Sutton's mouth crashed down on hers. With every insistent sweep of his tongue, with every sweet and heady taste of her, his pulse hammered and his cock hardened. He imagined hoisting her onto the counter and driving into her, finding out firsthand where her kink started and how hard she'd let him push her. The second kiss was hotter than the first. Once the embers started smoldering, it wouldn't be long before they ignited.

She kissed him back with the same hot need. By the time they ended the kiss, they were both breathing hard and staring at each other with something akin to shock.

Then London nestled the side of her face against his chest. "Okay. Wow. Normally I'd say, whoa, let's take a step back, but all I can think is I'd rather take a running step forward straight to my bedroom."

"In due time, darlin'."

"You busy right now? Or are you just out of condoms?"

He stroked her hair and smiled against the top of her head. After a bit he said, "Yeah, I'm out of condoms. Haven't needed them."

She lifted her head and looked at him. "What? A hot, built guy like you ain't getting any at all?"

"Nope. You said it's been four months for you? I've got you beat. It's been over nine months for me. Since before my accident."

London's skeptical gaze roamed over his face. "Are you just saying that to make me feel less shitty?"

"Why would you think that?"

She slid her hands up his chest and curled her fingers around his jaw. "Because you look like this."

He blushed. "Now you're just bein' ridiculous."

"You can't honestly tell me you don't have women hitting on you all the freakin' time."

"Not lately, bein's I've been holed up at home recovering. Ain't a lot of women prowling around my place. My dogs tend to run them off."

"Sutton. I'm serious."

"So am I." He counted to five. "Women don't want to see a man struggling to put himself back together. It's easier to go it alone. I found that out the hard way the first time." He tugged her hands away from his face, sidestepping her and the topic. "So is there a dance tonight?"

His abrupt subject change perplexed her. "Yeah, but I'd decided to skip it."

Sutton angled his head toward her box of jewelry supplies. "Got other plans?"

"Maybe." London pointed to the back of the camper. "Got a mattress that needs pounding. And darlin'"—she gave him a hungry, full-body perusal—"you look completely recovered to me."

"Much as I'd love to take you up on that offer, ain't gonna happen today."

"Why not?"

"Because even before my injury I wasn't the kind of guy to indulge in indiscriminate sex." That made him sound like a total pussy. He made light of it. "That's why they call me 'The Saint,' remember? Plus, I'm gonna make you at least buy me dinner first."

"There's a box of Corn Pops in the cupboard. And the milk is fresh." She waggled her eyebrows. "I'd totally give it away to you for free."

He laughed. "Taunting me won't change my mind."

"So saintly you is leaving *just* when it's starting to get interesting?"

"Yep. I said my piece. Come by tomorrow when you get done here. I'll be around." He picked up the clipboard and scrawled his address and phone number in the last box where she'd written—*D.L. A-ride.* "Didja get my joke?"

"Dial a ride? Yes. Not funny."

"I've heard that before too."

"What?"

"That I lack a sense of humor and I'm always too serious about everything. So with that..." He headed for the door.

London grabbed his hand. "Did I scare you off by being too aggressive? Is that why you're slinking outta here like a scalded cat?"

"No." He said, "No," again more forcefully when her eyes remained skeptical. "I like that you know what you want—I'll never judge you for that. This all happened fast. You kissed me once; I kissed you once. I'm guessing the heat between us surprised us both, and hot stuff, ain't no doubt there's an inferno between us just waiting to ignite. We both need to think about it and decide how far this is gonna go before it blows up in our faces. But it's not happening an hour after we reconnected. And not ten steps from a bed."

"For the record, can I say I hate that you're right?" She plucked up the clipboard and clutched it to her chest. "I didn't even like you an hour ago. Now I'm pissy that you won't test the bounce factor of my mattress, so obviously my head isn't clear."

"Lust and reason rarely go hand in hand." Sutton let his gaze move over her, making sure she knew he liked what he saw. "Let's let reason win today."

"Fine. But it doesn't feel like much of a victory."

"For me either, sweetheart."

After Sutton exited London's camper, he headed straight for his truck. Unlike past years on the rodeo circuit, no one stopped him to chat. No one recognized him. That would've bothered him when he'd been trying to make a name for himself. Now it just drove home the point he was done with the world of rodeo.

Or he would be, as soon as Dial had regained some of what he'd lost. Only then could Sutton find an owner that saw the workhorse beneath the spirited nature.

The drive to his place passed quickly. At home he fed Dial and talked to him about London, mostly out of habit. There were times on the road when Sutton had felt his horse was his only friend—totally fucked up, but true. Dial wasn't just a tool to him. Most of the time the opposite was true. Dial needed the challenge of those moments on the dirt. Sutton needed the moments on the dirt as a means to an end.

Over the years, socialization had gotten easier for him, but in the beginning on the circuit, he'd remained in the background, barely speaking because he'd always been painfully shy. Early on most folks considered him conceited, but he couldn't help people seeing what they wanted to. Rather than hit the wild parties after a competition, he hid in his horse trailer and watched DVDs.

That's not to say Sutton didn't have friends—just none of them, with the exception of Breck Christianson, were professional rodeo competitors. Plenty of buckle bunnies had sniffed around him from day one. But he'd understood early on that it wasn't him personally those women saw, but him as a meal ticket.

After Charlotte dumped him and he'd survived his recovery, he'd returned to life on the blacktop and lost some of his reserve. He hadn't gone hog wild as much as he'd learned to separate love from sex. Being in a serious relationship at such a young age hadn't given him any experience with no-strings-attached, let's-fuck-just-because-it-feels-amazing kind of sex and he quickly became a huge fan of it. But even then, his sexual exploits were nowhere near what his fellow road dogs were indulging in. And he'd yet to find a woman willing to let him explore his darker side. So, he'd let her set the initial parameters and then he'd push the sassy cowgirl's boundaries.

As he walked back up to his house from the corral, it reminded him how much he loved being at home. His house was his one indulgence. Basic on the outside. But inside? Big rooms, open space. A man his size needed room to move around. And because he'd had the house built from the ground up, he'd installed an underground shooting range. The basement, dug a level deeper than most, was literally his fortress. The concrete bunker that ran a 100 yards beneath his house was completely soundproofed and fully ventilated. He could fire ten clips from an AR-15 and anyone sitting in his living room wouldn't hear even a small pop.

His private shooting range wasn't something he broadcasted, lest he get called a gun nut or a freak preparing a bunker for the end of days—neither of which were true. But he'd always been drawn to guns. Not for hunting, not for collecting, but for the actual skill it takes in shooting all types of firearms. If he hadn't been offered a college scholarship for rodeo, he would've gone into the army. And he'd taken perverse pleasure in turning the indoor "dog run" that Charlotte insisted on for her stupid poodles into a regulation competitive shooting range with all the bells and whistles he could legally buy.

Not only had the shooting range saved his sanity during his recovery period this go around, but being home for longer than a week at a time, he'd had a chance to hang out with other guys with the same passion.

Passion. He'd had passion for his sport and passion for his hobby, but passion for a woman had been missing long before his accident.

It'd shocked him how quickly passion had sparked to life with London Gradsky today. He liked the challenge of her. His thoughts scrolled back to that day she'd given him what-for when she'd found out he'd bought Dial. The fire flashing in her eyes, the over-the-top hand gestures. He admired that she didn't hold back her true nature.

She might be used to getting her own way on the dirt, but guaranteed he didn't get roped into this situation without planning to take some risks of his own.

Chapter Four

Winning four steer wrestling world championships must've paid well because Sutton Grant had a gorgeous house. A ranch style with southwestern elements. The corral spanned the distance between the house and the big metal barn-like building on the left side. A three-car garage on the right side balanced out the sprawling structure.

It was obvious this house had no full-time female occupant. No flowers or landscaping beyond a few bushes beneath the front windows. The reverse U-shaped driveway was unique, giving her the choice to pull up to the garage, follow the wide swath of blacktop and park in front of the house or pull up to the metal outbuilding.

Before she could decide which would be the best parking option, Sutton strolled out the front door sans shirt. When she tore her gaze away from his muscled torso and saw he was wearing pants—pity that—and that he was barefoot, she hit the brakes hard. Nothing on earth was sexier than a bare-chested barefoot man in faded jeans. Nothing.

Sutton meandered over.

She unrolled her window but gazed straight ahead at the garage door instead of his mesmerizing chest.

"Hey. I wasn't expecting you so early."

"Did I interrupt something? Because I can come back."

"Why would you think you interrupted something?"

Because you're half-dressed and I'm pretty sure if I look down at your holy fuck washboard abs, I'll see the top button on your jeans is undone. Then I'll imagine you were lounging naked in bed when you heard a car pull up and you're probably commando beneath those body-hugging jeans.

Jesus. She even sounded like a breathless twit in her head.

"London. Why aren't you lookin' at me?"

"Because you've got way too few clothes on." *And I've got way too many ideas on what to do with a hot, half-naked man.*

A rough-tipped finger traced the length of her arm down from the ball of her shoulder, pausing to caress the crease in her elbow, and continuing down her forearm and wrist, stopping to sweep his thumb across her knuckles. "You could even things up, darlin'. Get rid of that pesky shirt and bra."

"I'm not wearing a bra," slipped out.

Sutton sucked in a sharp breath. "Prove it."

London's head snapped around so fast she might need to find a neck brace. Her indignation vanished when she saw his dimpled grin.

"That gotcha to look at me."

"Jerk."

Keeping his eyes on hers, he gently uncurled her fingers from her grip on the steering wheel. "Let's start over. Good afternoon, London. You're lookin' pretty today. I'm happy to see you. There's a concrete slab on the far side of the barn where you can park your camper."

"Thanks."

"You're welcome."

Sutton continued staring and touching just the back of her hand in a manner that should've been sweet but sent hot ripples of awareness vibrating through her. "Uh, I'll just go park now."

He released her hand and her eyes. "Need help?"

"Nah. I've done this a million times." She drove along the front of the house, cutting the turn wide when she started down the driveway. Then she put it in reverse and cranked it hard, perfectly lining it up alongside the building. After she climbed out of the truck, she saw Sutton had already unhooked the camper from the ball hitch. "Thanks."

"My pleasure. You wanna grab the stabilizer blocks?"

She lifted them out of the back of the truck and set them on the ground.

Sutton had them in place in seconds. Then he stood and brushed the dirt from his palms.

Her focus had stuck on how the muscles in his arms flexed. Given his bulked up state, it didn't look like the man had spent the last eight months recuperating from injuries.

"London?"

She met his amused gaze. "Did I say something?"

"Not with your mouth, darlin', but you are sayin' a whole lot with them burning hot eyes of yours."

"Sorry."

"Don't be. You need help hauling anything into the house?"

London frowned. "No. But if you'll show me where I can plug in—"

"No." Then Sutton crowded her, trapping her against the side of her camper with his arm right by her face. "I'm a single guy with a four-bedroom house. There's no reason for you to stay in your camper."

Good Lord his muscles were even more impressive this close up. What weight exercise did he do to get that deep cut in his biceps? She could probably stick her tongue halfway into that groove. Then she could follow that groove down... Way down.

Stop. Mentally. Licking. Him.

"London?"

She cleared her throat. "I can think of a reason."

"What?"

Scrambled by his nearness, she said, "I snore really loud."

"I'll wear earplugs."

"I get up at least twice every night to use the bathroom."

"You have a private bathroom in your room."

"I'm messy. Really messy."

"I have a housekeeper."

She was losing this battle. *Think, London, because if you can't come up with a plausible reason to stay out of his house, guaranteed you'll be in his bed.*

"That's what I'm hoping for."

Her gaze zoomed to his. "What are you hoping for?"

"That you'll end up in my bed. Or I'll end up in yours."

Jesus. She'd said that out loud.

Grinning, he pushed back. "Come on. I'll show you the guest room."

She followed him inside. The entrance opened up into a big foyer with tile floors. Beyond the pillars separating the entrance from the hallways going either direction, she saw a great room with a fireplace, a man-sized flat screen, and puffy couches. Windows overlooked a patio. The living area melded into an open kitchen and small dining room. No bachelor bland in Sutton's abode. The colors were masculine; rust, dark brown, and tan, yet the coffee table, dining room table and chairs, and end tables were light rough-sawn wood.

"What a gorgeous space. Did you decorate it?"

"Not on your life." He snagged a black wife beater off the back of the sofa and yanked it on over his head. "I told my mom what I wanted, well, mostly what I *didn't* want, and she supervised since I wasn't around much."

"She lives close by?"

"A few miles up the road. This house is actually on the far corner of the ranch."

"Handy."

"My brothers each have their own places too."

"There are worse things than having your family as your closest neighbors."

Sutton flipped a switch and light flooded the hallway. "We've never had a problem with it. What about you? I don't remember how many siblings you've got."

"Two. My older brother, Macon, is an attorney in Denver. My younger sister, Stirling, received her masters' degrees in biology, genetics, and animal science." London held her breath, waiting for the inevitable question. *What's your degree in?* Yeah, she bristled at being the lone Gradsky kid without a college education. Instead, she'd chosen the "school of hard knocks" route.

"So you're a middle child, too?"

She slowly exhaled. "Yep."

"My oldest brother, Wynton, ranches with our dad, as does my younger brother, Creston."

"Wynton, Sutton, Creston; masculine names for strapping western ranching sons."

He leveled her with a look. "I'd think a woman named London wouldn't poke fun."

"I'm not. What are your folk's first names?"

"Jim and Sue. Mom wanted something unique for us, but personally I'd rather be Bill or Bob or Joe." He took a few steps down the hallway. "Here's the bathroom."

"At least your mother didn't go with a theme. My dad's full name is Charleston Gradsky, and he hates it so he goes by Chuck. But that didn't deter Mom from picking a southern city as my brother's name."

"So you're London because she's Berlin? Why didn't she name your sister Paris?"

She whapped him in the arm. "Too easy. She narrowed her choices to Stirling, which is a town in Scotland, or Valencia, a town in Spain. She hated the idea that Valencia could be shortened to Val. God forbid one of her kids would have a somewhat normal name."

"Wynton never uses his full name. He's gone by Wyn since he started school. Same with Cres. But ain't no way to shorten Sutton."

"Or London."

They smiled at each other.

Sutton opened his mouth to say something then shook his head. He turned and started down the hallway. They passed two closed doors and he opened the third. "This is the guest room." He pointed. "Bathroom is through that door."

"This is really rice." The space was simple, tan walls with oak trim and oatmeal colored Berber carpet. Centered on the longest wall was a big brass bed sporting a Denver Broncos bedspread. Next to it was a nightstand with a matching orange and blue desk lamp. Opposite sat an antique dresser with a TV on top. Shades covered the windows, leaving the room cool and dark—just like she liked it. Some summer nights her camper was like sleeping in a tin can. "You've convinced me to crash here, although I'll point out it's a good thing I'm not a Kansas City Chiefs super fan."

"Bite your tongue, darlin'. Them's fightin' words."

She peeked into the bathroom. Same Broncos theme. When she looked at him again, she casually asked, "Where's your room?"

"At the other end of the hallway. There are two bedrooms on this side and two on that side." He smirked. "So yes, your room is as far from mine as it gets."

How was she supposed to respond? Good? Or that sucks?

"Need help unloading your stuff?"

"No. My stuff is scattered throughout my camper, and I need to dig it out first."

"Okay. If you need anything, holler." Then he left the room.

London used the facilities and figured out the bare minimum of what she'd need. She practically tiptoed down the hallway, leaving the front door unlatched so she wouldn't disturb Sutton with the door slamming.

She had packed a suitcase—full of dirty clothes—and set it outside hoping laundry privileges were included in her guest status. She unearthed a duffel bag and shoved the few clean clothes inside along with her makeup bag. Her laptop bag held all of her electronics and charging cords. Then she figured she'd need her boots and hat, which were in the back of her club cab. Since she'd be dealing with Dial, a notoriously stubborn horse, a crop would come in handy. She rooted around under the seat until she found it.

Looking at the pile, she wished she'd taken Sutton up on his offer of help. She slipped the strap of the duffel over her left shoulder and the laptop strap over the right. Hat on her head, boots teetering precariously on top of the zipped duffel, she reached for the suitcase handle.

"You'd rather sprain your damn neck than accept my help?"

She whirled around. Her hat, boots, and crop went flying. "Don't sneak up on me like that!"

Sutton picked up her riding crop and muttered, "I oughta use this on you."

"Okay."

He shot her a look.

She didn't break eye contact. Neither did he.

Then he offered her a mysterious smile, grabbed the suitcase and rolled it to the front door.

Whew. Talk about a hot moment. Scooping her hat onto her head, she trudged behind him. She met Sutton in the hallway. "When you're done getting settled, I'll be in the kitchen."

I don't know if I'll ever be settled around you.

Not only was he…oh, a fucking dream man with those looks, those eyes, that body, enough amazing attributes to make any man cocky, he rarely acted that way. If she didn't know better, she'd swear the man was…shy.

Nah. He couldn't be.

Why not? Why do you think you know him? You've met the man one time. You've heard your parents talk about him, but you've had exactly one hour-long conversation with him.

But he hadn't shied away from kissing her or from accepting her challenge to act like her boyfriend. And he'd all but told her she was crashing in his house, not her camper.

Those were the actions of a self-confident person, not the shy, retiring type.

Since when are those traits mutually exclusive?

Maybe she should stop staring at the closed door like an idiot, clean herself up, and go talk to him.

London changed from shorts into jeans. Hopefully the flies weren't bad and she wouldn't regret wearing a T-shirt instead of switching to a long-sleeved blouse. She tried to run a comb through her hair since she'd had the windows down on the way here, but the brush got stuck so she finger-combed it into a low ponytail. Not the best look, but she was headed into the pasture for the next couple of hours and bad hair days were why God had invented hats.

As she wandered down the hallway, she expected to hear the TV or maybe music, but the house remained quiet. She turned the corner into the kitchen and saw bags of groceries strewn across the quartz countertops. Whoa. That was a lot of food.

Sutton slammed the cupboard door and spun around. He seemed startled to see her. "Oh. There you are. That was fast."

She shrugged. "I travel light. And I'm not much of a primper anyway." Which is probably part of the reason her ex upgraded to a more feminine model. "What's all this food for? You having a party? Feeding an army?"

He ran his hand over the top of his head in a nervous gesture. "The food is for you, actually."

"All of it? Do I look like I eat like a fucking Broncos linebacker or something?" she asked sharply.

"No. Jesus." Bracing his hands on the counter, he hung his head. "Look. I suck at this kinda stuff, okay? I never have anyone stay with me, say nothin' of a woman. I figured I oughta stock up on girl food—yogurt, salad, fruit, diet soda, double-stuff Oreos—but I reached the checkout and realized I'd bought nothin' for me. Then I worried maybe you didn't like the stuff I'd picked so I ended up buying more. Now I'm staring at it, embarrassed as hell, knowing you'll see all this food and think I'm some kind of freak for assuming we'll eat together at all."

Oh yeah. The man really was shy and unsure. And very, very sweet, worrying how *she'd* take *his* thoughtfulness in providing food for her. Impulsively, she ducked under his arm and set her hands on his chest. "Sutton Grant. You are a saint and a total sweetheart, and forgive me for acting like a thankless dick."

"You're not upset?"

"Only that you'd assume I eat girl food. Dude, I'm meat and potatoes all the way." His heart thumped beneath her palm but he didn't touch her. "Then again, I eat salad and other healthy stuff so I can eat Oreos."

"I also bought cookies and cream ice cream."

She licked her lips. "Another fave of mine. I always say I'll have a little taste, but it never works out that way. I end up wanting more."

"I know how that goes," he murmured.

His gaze seemed stuck on her mouth.

As much as she wanted him to kiss her, she knew he wouldn't. Not without a clear sign from her. "How about I help you put these groceries away?"

He retreated. "I'd appreciate it."

"Then I'll head out and catch Dial and see where we're at."

Chapter Five

Dial proved to be his usual dickish self to London.

Which was a relief. Sutton half expected the gelding would make him look like a fool by being compliant.

London suggested Sutton stay on the outside of the corral that way Dial knew she was in charge.

It took her thirty minutes to catch him and put a halter on him. Dial didn't fight the saddle, but he needed the riding crop to get him moving.

For the next hour, he watched, mesmerized as London worked Dial over with a combination of firmness and a loving touch. He'd expected her to reward the horse with oats after she unsaddled him, removed the training bit and bridle, and thoroughly brushed him down. But she merely looked into his eyes and stroked his head as she spoke to him.

For once, Dial stood still.

Yeah, Sutton wouldn't move either if London had her hands all over him as she murmured in his ear.

Since the moment she'd driven up, her interest in him still apparent after he'd given her some time to think it over, he realized that pretending they were crazy about each other wouldn't be a problem.

London bounded across the corral, her dark ponytail swinging behind her. She was long and lean—it looked like a strong wind could knock her over, so it was hard to imagine her forcing her will on animals five times her size. He'd watched as she'd approached Dial, and her presence exceeded the size of her body.

She exited through the gate and he walked over to meet her halfway. "You all right?"

"Sore."

"Where?" he asked, alarmed.

"Don't worry. Just my arms and neck, nothing serious. Dial gets it in his head to resist and he pulls like a damn draft horse."

"You're welcome to use my hot tub if you think it'll help loosen your muscles."

London tipped her head back and squinted at him, raising her hand to block the sun. "You being a nice guy ain't an act, is it?"

"You run into guys like that? Where it's an act?"

"Guys who are assholes beneath the slicked up public persona? Yep. That's how most of them are."

Sutton started walking toward the house. "I didn't see the point in maintaining a public and a private face. If it wasn't for sponsor's requirements, I wouldn't have any public presence in the world of rodeo."

"So the perfect day at the rodeo for you?"

"Do my runs. Take my turn as a hazer. Collect my check and visit with the rodeo officials and coordinators. Hop in my truck and haul my horse home. Then have a beer on my back patio and reflect on my performance—whether I win or lose." He shot London a sideways glance. "Pretty boring, huh?"

"Not at all." When she looped her arm through his, he managed to keep his feet moving instead of stumbling over them. "Attitudes of entitlement among the rodeo participants is why I rarely take jobs with them. They want me to fix a horse in a day, when the problem's usually been years in the making. They've watched 'The Horse Whisperer' way too many times and they believe that shit is real."

"You mean that one session with Dial didn't cure him?"

"Not. Even. Close."

"Dammit. Way to dash my hopes. You're fired."

London hip-checked him.

They fell silent on the rest of the short walk, but London didn't pull away until they reached the patio. "This is such a great space. No neighbors, no traffic noises, no cattle. I could sit out here for hours and just enjoy the solitude."

"Hang tight. I'll grab us a couple of beers."

"Sounds good."

When Sutton returned, he saw that London had ditched her hat and her boots. With her face aimed toward the sky, her dark hair swaying in the breeze, a slight smile on those full lips and the sexy way she spread her toes out in the patch of sunshine, he was absolutely poleaxed. Not only by lust, but by the premonition this would be the first of many times they'd be together like this.

You wish.

When she opened her eyes and smiled at him, lust muscled aside any feelings of destiny. He ached to see her mouth wrapped around his cock. He wanted to see the diamond pattern from the metal table imbedded in her skin after he pinned her to it and fucked her hard.

"Sutton? You okay?"

"Yep." He handed her a Bud Light.

"This is perfect. Thank you."

He sipped and asked the question that'd been weighing on him. "So what's the deal with Dial?"

She expelled a long sigh. "He's got deep-seated anxiety about his ability to perform, not only to the level he's reached, but on any level at all. He feels he's being punished for a mistake that clearly wasn't his fault. And in horse years, that punishment seems like years instead of months. So he's resentful of you and the only way he can show that resentment is by not doing what you ask or demand of him."

Sutton's jaw dropped. "Are you freakin' kidding me?"

London laughed. "Of course I'm bullshitting you, bulldogger. Sheesh. That kinda psychobabble about a horse's psyche is a bunch of horseshit—pardon the pun. Dial hasn't been worked with for months. He's rusty. He's ornery. Does he miss being a workhorse and doin' what he was trained to do? No idea. Alls I can do is hope the training we both did over the years kicks in at some point." She swigged her beer. "It ain't a one day fix. But hell, maybe he'll snap back to it and he'll be ready to hit the dirt in a week."

There was his nightmare scenario.

She leaned forward and pulled a folded piece of paper out of her back pocket and dropped it in front of him. "Take a look at those numbers."

"What's this?"

"My rates."

He unfolded the paper. Stopped himself from whistling when he saw the amount. London Gradsky commanded a pretty penny for working with pretty ponies.

"Of course, I wrote that out yesterday before you offered me room and board."

"So do you need a pen so you can refigure the amount?" he teased.

"Nice try, but no. The dollar amount stays the same, but I'll double the amount of time I work with Dial until there are results."

"Sounds fair." He offered his hand and she shook it.

A meadowlark trilled and she smiled. "Your house is centrally located to how far I have to drive to my clients. I will be so glad not to have to leave my camper at a campsite."

"I'll be a snoopy bastard and ask why you've distanced yourself from

Grade A Farms. Your folks know about you living in your camper, parking at different campsites every night?"

"No. And please don't tell them." She paused. "My parents are great people. No complaints on the familial relationship. But their business goals are different than mine. They breed horses and sell them. They're shrewd in that they demand stud and genetic shares from those sales, but refuse to get into the sperm collecting and artificial insemination portion of the business. For a while they were trying to fit each high-end horse to the specific rodeo discipline. I was all for that."

"They don't do that anymore?"

"Nope."

"What happened?"

"My big shot lawyer brother stuck his nose in. He created a spreadsheet that showed how much money they lost in a five-year period by doing it that way and cross referenced it with the number of national champions who were using Grade A livestock to compete. They were losing capital for a few lousy bragging rights. They revamped their policies, which is why they had no issue selling Dial to you."

"So you weren't really pissed off at me for suggesting they castrate Dial?"

"Oh, I was plenty pissed off at you about that. I'd had my sights set on breeding him with a gorgeous paint. She was sturdy, sweet-tempered, and would've done fine with the beast mounting her. Anyway, that was when I knew I had to fully strike out on my own. While some aspects of what I do are still the same, I'm not in the same place, day in, day out. My clients are varied, not just monied rodeo stars. Plus, I've tried other training disciplines, not just the ones my dad used." London nudged his knee with her foot. "You played a part in me making that decision."

"Then I think I deserve a deeper discount on your services."

She laughed. "Don't push your luck."

Sutton stood and held out his hand. "Time to earn your keep, whip cracker."

London took his hand without hesitation. "Which is what?"

"Helping me get supper on the table."

* * * *

Later that night they sat side by side on the swing on the patio, watching the flames crackle in the fire pit.

They'd shared a meal together, cleaned up together, and talked about everything under the sun, except rodeo and horses. Sutton expected she'd bring up the other part of their deal, acting like a couple. One thing he hadn't been clear on was whether they were telling their families they were involved or if the only place they were "out" was on the weekends at the fairgrounds. The other thing he needed to know? If London was trying to get Stitch back. He was onboard to help London save face, but he wouldn't be happy if she planned on returning to her ex. He'd played the chump before.

But as the evening wore on, he hadn't asked because it'd been easy— ridiculously so—how well they got along.

Maybe because they were both on their best behavior. Maybe it was something else that Sutton was too superstitious to name. Tempting to let this easy camaraderie lie, but he needed to know exactly where he stood with her. "Did you see Stitch and Paige last night or today?"

"No. I pretty much avoided everyone. Stayed in my camper and worked on some jewelry."

"Why?"

"I figured a few people saw that kiss at the rodeo grounds and I didn't want to explain it. Or you. I wanted to make sure we were on the same page—hah! Poor word choice, being on *that* Paige since that's now Stitch's job—before we put ourselves out there in public."

He nodded.

"So I'm really grateful you opened up your home and we can get to know each other as friends."

Fuck. There was the word he'd feared. "Friends?" he repeated. She sure as fuck hadn't wanted to be friends when she'd practically tackled him to her bed.

"Yeah. I mean you were right to put the brakes on us yesterday. I'm more impulsive in my personal life than I should be. Just like you said, you're the calm, quiet voice of reason. So if we spend this week getting to know each other, on, ah—another level, our relationship will seem less suspicious this weekend when we're together."

"Less like we're literally doin' a horse trade to get something that each of us wants?"

She laughed. "Exactly. Being friends puts us more at ease."

"Because it's all about appearances." That came out with a bitter edge.

"It has to be. I don't want to get caught in a lie. Wouldn't that be the most mortifying thing you can think of?"

No, the most mortifying thing I can think of is getting friend-zoned by you in the first four hours of play.

Damn. No wonder he didn't put himself out there. Good thing he'd asked about their parameters before he'd made a move.

But Sutton had to respect her for taking the time to consider her boundaries when she clearly had none yesterday. Yet, the bottom line for him hadn't changed. He needed London to work his horse—no matter how much he wanted to work her over in his bed nine ways to Sunday.

Friends. He could do that. Hell, he oughta be used to it by now.

But fuck if he wasn't tired of denying himself, even when it was his own damn fault. Demanding she stay with him in his house. Cooking for her. What people said about him was true. He was too damn nice and accommodating, but he did have an ulterior motive—hot kinky sex. But he didn't want London to feel obliged to fuck him, which sounded ridiculous in his head and would sound even more idiotic if he said it out loud. He needed to retreat, regroup, before he stuck his boot in his mouth.

Sutton forced a yawn and then stood. "Sorry. It's getting late."

London's eyebrows shot up. "Late? It's only eight-thirty."

Shit. "Huh. Well, it seems later than that which is a sign I should call it a night."

"Oh. Well. Sure. Do you mind if I stay up and wash some dirty clothes?"

"Help yourself to whatever you need."

"Thank you. I was afraid I'd be walking around naked tomorrow morning since everything I own is dirty."

Do not think about naked and dirty and London in the same sentence.

Friends, remember?

Repeat it. F-r-i-e-n-d-s.

Still, this was gonna be a long damn week.

Chapter Six

Now London understood why people called Sutton Grant "The Saint."

She'd been trying to get under his skin—okay mostly she'd been trying to get into his Wranglers—for the past four days and the man hadn't been tempted even once, as far as she could tell.

They spent their free time together. She stuck close while he cooked supper, tasting and touching and forcing him to feed her little tidbits. She wore pajama short shorts and a camisole that showed a lot of her skin when they watched TV. When he'd mentioned suffering from a sore neck, she'd offered to give him a massage, but he'd spoken of the personal massager his therapist had lent him. When she'd noticed his razor-stubbled face and volunteered to shave off the scruff, he'd just smiled and said he'd pick up razors next time he went to town.

A saint.

But...London knew he watched her. He watched her work with Dial—from a distance. He watched for her truck to pull into the drive at the end of her workday—from a distance. He watched her doing beadwork—from a distance. But he watched her watching TV up close and personal. He watched her all the damn time.

But that's all the man did. Watched.

What the hell was he waiting for?

Maybe he's been watching you for some sort of sign.

She'd had a huge fucking neon sign over her head from the moment they'd met that flashed "Available Now!" What more did he need?

Maybe he's not attracted to you.

Wrong. She'd felt his attraction when he'd kissed her. It'd been hard to miss or ignore as it'd dug into her belly.

Maybe he wants to stick to your business deal.

So he was saving his performance for the weekend when he'd have to be all over her?

Performance. Why did that word turn her stomach? Because she wanted it to be more? To be real?

It'd felt real on Saturday as those amazing eyes of his had eaten her up the way she knew his mouth wanted to. It'd felt real on Sunday, seeing his shy, flirting side behind the serious persona. But Monday morning he'd acted buddy-buddy—she'd half expected him to give her a noogie—and it'd been that way between them ever since, no matter how much she tried to turn the sweet saint into a red-hot sinner.

After London parked at Sutton's place, she opted to keep her sour mood to herself and headed straight for the corral rather than stopping inside the house first.

The day had turned out to be a scorcher. She stripped out of her long-sleeved shirt to just her camisole. Grabbing her tack out of the barn, she draped it over the metal railing. She looped the rope around her neck and whistled twice, surprised when Dial came trotting over. They played catch and mouse for a bit, not in an ornery way, but playful and she was happy to see the reappearance of that side of the horse.

This first week she'd planned on earning Dial's trust. He'd balked but each day he made a baby step. Pushing too hard too fast caused backsliding into familiar behavior.

Maybe that's what's going on with Sutton. You're pushing a man to get what you want. What if that's not what he wants?

She'd get to the bottom of it tonight.

Since Dial had shown improvement, London decided to treat him with some oats. She'd sprinkled too many in the bucket and reached in to scoop some back out when Dial tried to crowd her to get his face in the bucket.

"Hey, rude boy, back off." She turned to move the bucket aside and she felt a sharp, hard nip on her upper arm. "Motherfucking son of a whore!" She swung the bucket up and dropped it on the other side of the fence. Something hot and wet flowed down her arm. She expected to see horse slobber but it was blood.

So much for the old wives' tale about horses bolting at the scent of blood. Dial just stared at her, unmoving, his tail flicking back and forth, trying to intimidate her.

Fuck that.

London rose up, making herself as big as possible, staring him right in the eyes. "Back off," she said sharply. "Now."

Dial backed up.

She walked over to where she'd left her shirt. Her arm stung. Small, hard horse bites hurt worse than anything, tender flesh caught between that powerful jaw. It'd been a while since a bite had broken the skin.

"London?"

Shit, shit, shit. She'd hoped she could get inside and cleaned up before seeing Sutton. No such luck.

"What's wrong?" He tried to grab her injured arm to spin her around and she hissed at him, cradling her elbow with her hand. "What the hell happened?"

"Dial bit me."

"Lemme see."

"Not a big deal. It'll be fine once it's cleaned out."

"Let me fucking see it, London. Now."

She glanced up at him.

Fury blazed in his eyes when he saw the blood. "Let's go inside and I'll take a closer look." He gently lifted her arm until it was parallel with her shoulder. Then he grabbed her shirt from her free hand and held it beneath the bite to catch the blood. "Hold it like this. Did he get you anywhere else?"

"He's not like a wolf or a dog with sewing machine teeth that just keep attacking. One chomp and that's it."

Muttering something, he looked over at the corral then back at her. "Come on."

Sutton kept his hand on top of hers beneath the wound as he led her into the house through the patio door. She expected he'd stop in the kitchen but he directed her down the hallway opposite of her wing, into his bedroom. She got an image of heavy wood furniture before she found herself in a large bathroom.

He seated her on the toilet—the lid had already been down, an extra point for that—and propped her forearm on a towel on the countertop. "How bad does it hurt?"

"You don't need to make a big deal about this. And don't worry. I won't cry."

Then Sutton was right in her face. "You don't have to be the tough chick with me. Now tell me how bad it hurts."

"It stings. Worse than my foot getting tromped on but not as bad as getting bucked off and landing on my ass."

"That's a starting point." He pushed a loose hank of hair behind her ear. "Sit tight while I dig out my first aid kit."

While Sutton rummaged in a tall cabinet, she checked out the space. No bland white fixtures, tiles, or vanity in here. Gray cabinets with black accents. The countertop was black, the sinks were gray. The walls of the glass-fronted walk-in shower were frosted, but behind that she could see the walls were speckled with the same color scheme. The space was wholly masculine yet classy.

"You ready for me to clean this out and gauge the damage?" he asked softly.

"Shouldn't I ask for your medical qualifications first?"

"Helicopter medic in 'Nam. Did two tours in the medical corps during the Gulf War, then a stint in Iraq and Afghanistan."

London smiled. "And some people say you don't have a sense of humor. Wait, is it considered bathroom humor if you actually crack jokes in the bathroom?"

"Now who's the funny one? So it's okay if I poke around?"

"Take off your belt so I have something to bite down on."

She watched as he uncapped a bottle of antiseptic. Every muscle in her body tightened.

"You weren't kiddin' about needing the strap, were you, darlin'?"

Whoa. She could take that the wrong way—but so could he. She said nothing and shook her head.

"Maybe you'd better look away and focus on something else."

London locked onto the visage that'd distract her—Sutton's handsome face. She knew he'd shaved this morning but dark stubble already coated his cheeks, jaw, and throat. She'd fallen into a fantasy where he left beard burns on her throat as he ravished her when he said, "Doin' okay?"

"I guess." She hissed at the stinging spray.

"This stuff will kick in soon and it has a numbing agent."

"How bad does it look? Is the skin flapping so I'll need stitches?"

"No. The bleeding's mostly stopped now." He pressed a gauze pad over the mark.

"Fuck that stings."

"Almost done."

The way he said it... "No, you're not. And if that's the case? I'd rather sit on the counter than the toilet. Then you won't have to bend down and get a crick in your neck." She stood before he could argue. But he curled his hands around her hips and hoisted her up. She automatically widened her knees so he could step between them.

When he reached for her arm, the backs of his knuckles brushed the outside of her breast and her nipple immediately puckered. Because Sutton had his head angled down, she couldn't tell if he'd noticed or not.

But she noticed everything about him. The scent of clean cotton mixed with the darker scent of oil emanating from beneath his starched collar. His full lips were parted as he concentrated on his task, but his breathing stayed steady. She wanted to run her fingers through his dark hair, trap his beautiful face in her hands and suck on those lips until his mouth opened for her kiss. Whisper secrets in his ear while his hair teased her cheek.

Mostly she wanted to ask the question that'd been burning on her tongue for days.

Do it.

"Are you ever going to make a move on me?"

That caught his attention. "What?"

"That wasn't a question to be answered by another question. Just tell me the truth."

Sutton lifted his head. "Where's this coming from, *friend?*"

Hey, was that sarcastic? She squinted at him. "It's coming from the fact we're supposed to be acting like boyfriend and girlfriend and you haven't kissed me or touched me beyond a friendly pat since we were in the camper, and I'm pretty sure kissing and petting is something we need to practice. A lot. So to recap, you haven't touched me since Saturday. It is now Wednesday."

"I know what day it is, London," he said testily.

"Oh yeah? Do you know what I call it? Hump day."

Silence as Sutton taped a chunk of gauze over the bite.

"I thought you'd at least crack a smile at that."

"It's really fucking hard to smile when you're bleeding in my bathroom because my douche-nozzle horse took a bite of you. Sometimes I think that nasty motherfucker deserves to spend his life isolated, and I don't know why I give a shit that he's properly trained since I'd like to ship him off to the damn glue factory."

"He didn't do it on purpose," she said softly.

His angry eyes finally met hers. "The fuck he didn't."

Seeing that fierceness? For *her?* Immediate lady boner.

"Can I tell you a secret, Sutton?"

"What?"

And then she couldn't do it. Couldn't tell him that Dial had shown remarkable progress in just four days. Because if she told him that...then what was his incentive to keep her here?

None.

She couldn't take that chance.

Even if she just had one quick run-in with Stitch this weekend, he'd see firsthand that she wasn't crying in her camper over him. That she'd hooked up with a hot man who sometimes stared at her—when he thought she wasn't looking—like he'd already stripped her naked and was fucking her over the back of his couch.

If it made her a douche-nozzle to fantasize about the shock on her ex's face when he realized his loss was a better man's gain, then so be it; she'd take it.

"London?"

"I like the way you say my name. Classy and dignified, with a hint of sexiness. Makes me wonder how it'd feel to have your mouth on me when you moan it."

"Jesus, London, knock it off."

She frowned. "Okay, that wasn't sexy at all."

"I'm not trying to be sexy with you right now," he snarled—in a decidedly sexy way, not that she'd point that out.

"You should be!" She poked him in the chest. "We're in *lurve*, remember? We are in the throes of a new relationship and that means we oughta be talking about fucking all the time."

"Do you always say the first damn thing that pops into your head?" he demanded.

"Pretty much. No reason to beat around the bush when you could be touching my bush, if you get my drift. See, alls I'd have to do is scoot my butt to the edge of this counter and you could slide inside me. After we're done eating supper, you could spread me out on the dining room table and have me for dessert." She allowed a small smile. "Or I could have you."

"Is there a point to your teasing?"

"That's the thing," she mock-whispered. "I'm not teasing."

While he stood staring at her—*through* her really—she saw his eyes darken as he imagined the exact scenarios she'd just detailed. Then his eyes turned conflicted and a little frosty. "Bullshit."

"What?"

"You're bein' a cock tease. You said you wanted to be *friends*, remember? Wasn't what I wanted, wasn't what I thought you wanted, but I've stuck to those parameters. So we're friends. But every damn time you touch me or get close to me and say such blatantly sexual things, the last goddamn thing I'm thinking about is bein' your friend. I'm a man, not a fucking saint, as I've heard you mutter loud enough for me to hear. You bein' all cute, flirty, funny, and sweet ain't helping me keep the parameters *you* set Sunday night."

Her jaw dropped. "*That's* what you got from our conversation Sunday night? That I just wanted to be friends with you?"

"How else was I supposed to take it?"

"Like it was the talk you demanded we have *before* we got involved on any level! That we'd discuss it. I said *friends* because I didn't think you'd appreciate me saying I'd rather ride *you* all damn night than your horse. And you jumped to the conclusion that *all* I wanted to be with you was friends? Bullshit. You ran away and pouted, bulldogger, when you jumped up and went to bed."

"What should I have done instead?"

"This." London curled her hand around the back of his neck and pulled his mouth to hers. No sweet kiss, no teasing. She fucked his mouth with her tongue like she wanted him to fuck her body. A hot, wet, drawn-out raw mating.

Sutton clamped his hand on her ass and jerked her to the edge of the counter, pressing his groin to hers. Kissing her without pause, holding her in place so he could ravage her mouth and her throat.

After his lips blazed a trail to her nipple, and he sucked on it through the fabric of her cami, she pulled back. "Tell me, bulldogger. Does that feel like I just wanna be friends with you?"

"No. Now give it back. I'm not done with it."

She started to laugh, but it turned into a moan when he pinched the wet tip with his fingers as his mouth reclaimed hers.

Holy hell could the man kiss. And touch. And rub and grind and get her so hot and bothered with her clothes on that she might've had a teeny orgasm right there.

Four loud raps sounded on his outer bedroom door, followed by, "Sutton? Come on. Dad's waiting in the truck."

Sutton froze. Then he broke the kiss and gazed into her face. Any chance she'd had of making light of the situation evaporated when she saw the sexual heat smoldering in those turquoise eyes.

When he brought his thumb up and traced the lower swell of her lip, the intensity pouring from this man might've set off another mini O.

"Sutton? Who's at the door?"

"Cres. We're taking Dad out to the Moose Club for poker night."

"Shouldn't you get going?"

"Yeah. In a minute." He pressed a kiss to her lips, then her chin, then her cheeks. "I'll be back late."

That's when she knew they were done for tonight—all night. She hopped down from the counter. "Thanks for the first aid. I'll go lie down now, but have fun with your family and I'll see you in the morning."

London pushed him out of his bathroom and locked the door.

Let him meet his brother with a hard-on. It'd serve him right for being an idiot.

Friends. What the hell had he been thinking?

* * * *

Sutton's cell phone rang on his nightstand early the next morning, yanking him from a hot dream where he'd taken London up on her offer of an after-dinner treat—except in his version they were on the rug in front of his fireplace, him having his dessert while she also had hers. Sixty-nine usually didn't appeal to him, but in his dream, he didn't have to concentrate on both giving and receiving pleasure—just being naked with her was the pleasure. Warm skin beneath his hands, her skilled mouth, the long trail of her hair teasing up the inside of his thighs...

His phone kept buzzing.

He answered, "Yeah?"

"Grant? It's Ramsey."

Ramsey? Why the hell was his shooting buddy calling him so early? "Do you know what the fuck time it is?

"Seven. I thought you ranching/cowboy types were up when the cock crows."

"I'm not a rancher, as you well know, so fuck off."

Ramsey laughed.

"What's up? Is your shooting range under fire?"

"Ha. Ha. You're fucking hilarious first thing in the morning."

"Why else would you be calling me? Wait. Are you offering your favorite customers free day passes?"

"You wish. And you're more than just a customer." Ramsey paused. "Look, this might seem like it's coming outta the blue but the truth is we both know that we've skirted this subject for months, so I'll just say it straight out. You're dealing with some heavy shit as far as getting back on track with your career. I recognize restless, man. So I'm not convinced that you want to return to that life on the road."

Sutton had no idea where this conversation was coming from. Wasn't like he'd gotten shitfaced with Ramsey and spilled his guts.

Maybe your lack of enthusiasm about returning to rodeo isn't as disguised as you believe. Your brothers mentioned the same thing in passing. More than once. "Now you've got my attention."

"I appreciate every time you've pitched in and helped out at the gun range. I've hinted around that I could use you on a part-time basis. You've been polite but vague on whether you'd seriously consider it. So maybe you won't give a damn, but I've run into a tricky situation, hence the early morning call."

"What situation?"

"My full-time range master, Berube, got orders and he's being deployed in a month. His deployment will last a year. That leaves me short a range master."

"Which makes me feel your pain as a customer and your friend, but why are you telling me?"

"Because you're an expert shot. You're very knowledgeable about guns without being a know-it-all asshole or a reckless dick."

"But I'm not a range master."

"You'd be a shoo-in to pass the range master's exam—the firearms range testing portion anyway. There's also a written test, but since you've earned a college degree, I'm sure that won't be a problem either."

Ramsey didn't hand out praise lightly, and Sutton found himself feeling proud of something for the first time in months.

"It's short notice, I know, but I'd planned a boys' night out for my instructors at my cabin to discuss the future growth of the gun range. Every guy who works for me will be there, so if you're even remotely interested in the position, this'd be the ideal time to get answers directly from the ones who work with me."

"Just one night? Or an all weekend thing?" He couldn't flake out on London. She expected him to play his part as her boyfriend.

"Just one night. Weekends are our busiest time so we'll be back at work tomorrow."

Two knocks sounded on the door. Then it opened and London walked in.

More like she sashayed in, wearing a see-through flimsy black thing that left nothing to the imagination. He could make out every muscled inch of her toned legs, the slight flare of her hips. Her flat belly and defined abs. Strategically placed bows hid her nipples but not the sweet curve of her tits.

"Sutton? I hope I'm not interrupting. I heard you talking in here so I assumed you were up. Look, I can't figure out the coffee pot. It keeps beeping at me every time I hit start."

Mostly Sutton heard, *blah blah blah* which translated to, "Look at my perky tits," followed by *blah blah blah*, "look at these naughty red panties that barely cover my pussy," and then *blah blah blah*, "look at my sexy bedhead and imagine holding this tangled hair in your fists while I suck your cock."

Fuck me. *Fuck me twice.*

"What the hell? Did you just tell me to fuck off?"

His rational train of thought had hit a fucking brick wall named London Gradsky.

"Sorry, no, I didn't say that. Gimme five minutes and I'll call you right back." Sutton tossed the phone on his bed without checking to see if he'd actually ended the call. "What. In. The. Name. Of. All. That's. Holy. Are. You. Doing. Half. Fucking. Naked. In. My. Bedroom?"

"I told you! Were you even listening to me?"

Not the words falling from your mouth when your body is speaking its own language loud and clear. He cleared his throat. "I was on the phone, so I missed most of what you'd said. What's the problem?"

"Your coffee pot hates me. I can't figure it out."

"I'll be right there after I slip some pants on." And after he whacked off so she didn't see how hopeful his dick was at seeing a hot, half-naked woman in his room first thing in the morning.

"Fine."

She turned to flounce out and he noticed she wore a thong. So she treated him to a full look at that perfect ass of hers before the crabby, horny man inside him yelled out, "And you'd better put some damn pants on too!"

Even with morning wood it only took him a minute to rub one out in the shower. He brushed his teeth and packed his overnight bag before he exited his room.

In the kitchen, he was both relieved and annoyed to see London had donned a robe.

"Took you long enough," she groused. "You've had coffee ready for me every day this week, so I don't think you understand the importance of coffee in my life. I'm a bitch on wheels without my morning caffeine fix."

"I saw the poor, unfortunate coffee maker that failed to do your bidding, so I'm aware of your demands. Watch and learn." He dumped the beans in and set the lid on the filter basket. "Line up these arrows. This is a grind and brew model. If the arrows aren't lined up, then it won't work at all."

"Oh. Thanks. Now it makes sense."

He smothered a yawn. "You're welcome."

"What time did you get home last night?"

"Late. Dad likes to cut loose on poker night. Especially if he wins. If I'd gotten home earlier, I planned on..." His gaze swept over her, from bedhead to pink-tipped toes. "Never mind what I'd planned 'cause it's a moot point now. That phone call earlier was a reminder that I have a prior commitment. So I'll be gone all day and tonight."

"But you *will* be back by tomorrow? You're coming to the Henry County Fair and Rodeo with me this weekend?"

"Yes. But I'll have to meet you there."

"Promise?"

He scowled. "I'm a man of my word, London."

She scowled back at him. "You'd better be. And where are you going on such short notice anyway?"

Away from temptation. At least for one night. While I figure out why in the hell I like you so much and I've only known you five days. And why that make-out session last night in my damn bathroom was more erotic than any sex I've had in years. "I'm headed out for a retreat."

"A spiritual retreat? Is that why they call you 'The Saint?'"

Sutton rolled his eyes. "I'm called 'The Saint' because I carried a Saint Christopher medallion my grandmother gave me when I first joined the pro tour. The guys saw it and ragged on me endlessly."

"Good to know. I'm assuming the name fit your lifestyle back then?"

"At first they tried calling me 'The Monk' but it didn't stick."

"Why not?"

He pinned her with a look. "Because there's a big difference between bein' a saint and a monk. And newsflash, darlin'... I'm neither."

Flustered, London poured a cup of coffee while the pot still brewed. "How's your arm today?"

She faced him and shrugged. "Doesn't feel too bad."

"So you're working with Dial this morning?"

"That's what I get paid to do."

His cell phone rang again. He checked the caller ID. Ramsey. Impatient bastard. He tucked his phone in his pocket. "I've got to go. Do you need anything before I do?"

"No."

"You're sure? No issues locking up?"

"I've been in a house in the country by myself before, Sutton."

If she'd shown any fear, he'd open up the locked door and assure her that she was far better protected than she could fathom.

"Wait. There is one thing I want."

When Sutton's eyes met the heat in hers, he knew exactly what she wanted. To avoid temptation, he curled his hands around the straps of his duffel bag and took two steps backward. "I can't. Not now."

"Why not?"

"Because the second I put my hands and mouth on you, we ain't goin' anywhere for the rest of the day. And night. We may even miss the entire Henry County Fair."

A sexy smirk curled her lips. "Then you'd better get going."

Chapter Seven

After London had loaded up her camper and hit the road toward Henry County Fairgrounds, she'd had way too much time to think. And all her thoughts were focused on one super-hottie, Sutton Grant.

Like...what did he do during the day? He wasn't involved in his family's ranching operation. Did he obsessively work out, trying to speed up his rehab and return to competition form? Because heaven knew, the bulldogger had the most banging body she'd ever seen up close and personal. Well, sort of up close and personal. Not that she'd gotten to do more than drool over his sculpted chest, arms and abs, even when the tempting man walked around his house half-naked.

She pondered other things Sutton could be doing with his time. Doing pay-per-view porn in his bedroom? Yeah, she'd pay to see that. Or maybe he was just watching XXX Websites all day. Maybe he played video games. She'd met her fair share of guys who were addicted to their X-box or PlayStation.

Why don't you just ask him?

Yeah, that'd go over well since he'd been so forthcoming about where he was going.

London froze. Wait a damn minute. Had Sutton been purposely vague because he'd set up a bootie call and didn't want her to know? Every time his cell phone rang this week, he'd excused himself to take the call in private.

But hadn't he told her that he hadn't been with a woman since his accident?

And you believed him? A harsh, sarcastic bark of laughter echoed in her head. *Because no man has ever lied about sex.*

Dammit. Had he played her?

Since Stitch had dumped her, she'd second-guessed everything about her attractiveness to the opposite sex, her personality, her sexual skills, and how she conducted herself on a professional level. In her twenty-seven years she'd never been the type of woman who needed validation from a man or a relationship to feel worthy of either.

Sutton Grant had better fall in line. Because he needed her more than she needed him.

* * * *

London had arrived early enough to score a primo parking place in the area specifically marked for rodeo contestants, stock contractors, exhibitors, and vendors. Being part of "tent city" was one of her favorite things about summer rodeo season. Nothing like sitting in front of a bonfire, drinking beer, laughing and talking about horses, rodeo, and the western way of life with other likeminded souls.

She tidied up the camper, deciding if Sutton showed, she'd let him sleep in the bed tonight since his big body wouldn't fit on the convertible sleeping area up front. But she'd be lying if she wasn't hoping they'd share that lumpy mattress sometime this weekend.

Then she changed into an outfit that made her feel sexy and desirable—a sleeveless lavender shirt embellished with purple rhinestones, her beloved b.b. simon crystal encrusted belt, her Miss Me jeans with black studded leather angel wings on the back pockets, and a pair of floral stitched Old Gringo cowgirl boots. She fluffed her hair, letting it fall in loose waves around her shoulders. After applying heavier makeup and a spritz of tangerine and sage perfume, she exited the camper.

The heat of the day hung in the air but the lack of humidity made it bearable. Still, an icy cold beer would make it better. London bought a bottle of Coors and wandered through tent city to see who was around.

The second person she ran into was Mel. "Hey, girl. If I'd known you were already here I'da brought you a frosty beverage."

Mel smiled and kept brushing down her palomino. "It's okay. I've gotta run Plato a bit so I'll take a rain check."

"Deal." London sipped her beer and looked around.

"Please don't tell me you're here so you can spy on Stitch and Paige."

London snorted. "As if. I don't give a hoot about them."

"Since when?"

"Since you told me I needed to get laid. A new guy barged into my life and swept me off my feet last weekend."

Mel stopped brushing Plato's back. "Are you kidding me?"

"Nope. He's hot, he's sweet, and he's crazy about me." London said a little prayer: *don't you let me down Sutton Grant, or so help me God I will superglue your dick and balls together in your sleep.*

"Uh-huh," Mel said skeptically. "But this guy that's so hot for you isn't from around here, is he? So I can't meet him."

"Wrong. He'll be here." She hoped.

Before Mel could demand more details, Stitch's best friend Lee—nicknamed Lelo on the circuit because of his association with Stitch—meandered over. He still wore his back number from the slack competition. "Hey Mel."

"Lelo. How's it hanging?"

"They ain't dangling low at all when I see you. They're high and tight and raring to go."

Mel muttered something.

When it became obvious to Lelo that Mel didn't intend to banter with him, he looked at London. "Hey. What's up?"

"Not much. What's up with you?"

"Askin' around, seein' where the parties are tonight."

A challenge danced in Mel's eyes. "Really, Lelo? Because I heard that Stitch and Paige were having a *huge* party at their campsite before the fireworks kicked off."

Lelo's mouth opened. Then snapped shut.

"I thought maybe you'd come by to invite me personally," Mel continued.

He looked between Mel and London. "Well, I, ah—"

"And since London is here, it'd be rude of you not to include her in that invite, doncha think?"

Jesus, Mel was a shit-stirrer sometimes. And precisely the reason they got along like gangbusters.

"I don't know if that's such a good idea, Mel, bein's they...dammit, you know why I can't invite her," Lelo blurted.

"Because London and Stitch used to date?" Mel flashed her teeth at London. "Water under the bridge, Lelo, since my girl here has herself a new boyfriend."

Shut your face, Mel, shut it right fucking now.

Lelo's eyes went comically wide—as if he hadn't considered that a possibility.

Which pissed London off. Big time.

"You don't say?" he said to London. "I thought you were still—"

"Hung up on Stitch?" Mel supplied. "Huh-uh. That's some bullshit Stitch and Paige have been spreading around so people don't hate him because he fucked London over."

"Mel," London warned.

"What? I'm sick of Opie and Dopie hinting around that you're some broken-hearted chump. Girlfriend, you are hot as lava and you were always way, way above Stitch's pay grade."

Lelo's focus bounced between them like he was watching a volleyball match. Then he said, "So who is this fella you're seein'? Anyone we know?"

Just then someone shouted her name. Someone with a deep, sexy voice.

London sidestepped Lelo and looked down the walkway between the horse trailers. There he was. The quintessential cowboy. And he stood less than fifty yards away. "Sutton?"

"Whatcha waiting for, darlin'? C'mere and gimme some sugar." He held his arms open.

Grinning, she ran toward him. He caught her and spun her in a circle before settling his mouth over hers. She twined her arms around his neck and gave herself over to his kiss.

And what an intoxicating kiss it was. His mouth teased, seduced, inflamed. By the time he eased back to brush tender kisses over her lips and jaw, her entire body shook.

Sutton whispered, "Sorry I'm late."

She nuzzled his neck, wishing she could pop open the buttons on his shirt and get to more skin. "You're here now."

"Did you think I wouldn't show?"

"The thought had crossed my mind."

He forced her to look at him. And her knees went decidedly weak staring into those crystalline eyes of his. "I said I'd be here. I'm a man of my word, London."

Sliding her arms down, she flattened her palms on his chest. "But when you left yesterday morning, you acted pissed off. So what was I supposed to think?"

"That I'm a man of my word," he repeated. He curled his hand around her jaw, denying her the chance to look away. "Ask me why I left my own damn house."

"Why'd you leave?"

"Because my willpower to finish the 'friends' conversation vanished the instant you showed up in my room wearing them baby doll pajamas that oughta be illegal, looking so fucking cute and sexy I had to sneak into my bathroom and whack off before I taught you how to use the coffee maker."

Her mouth dropped open.

"Surprised?"

"Very. You've seemed so...unaffected."

A growling noise rumbled from him before his mouth descended and he kissed the life out of her. She was so damn dizzy when he finally relinquished her lips, she had to fist her hands in his shirt just to keep from toppling over.

Then his breath was hot in her ear, sending shivers down the left side of her body. "Does that seem unaffected to you, sweetheart?"

"Ah. No."

"Good. Maybe you oughta offer me a little reassurance this ain't one sided."

London wreathed her arms around his neck and played with the hair that fell to his nape. "I've left my door cracked open every night, hoping you'd see an open door as an open invitation. I imagined the look on this gorgeous face if you caught me diddling myself."

His eyes darkened. "What did you imagine me doin' if I caught you?"

"Barging in, tying my hands to the brass headboard and driving me crazy with my vibrator before you pounded me into the mattress like you'd promised."

Another low-pitched growl reverberated against her skin. "You and me are gonna get a few things straight tonight. But probably not until after I fuck you hard at least once and swat your ass for you ever doubting me."

Sutton swallowed her gasp with another bone-melting kiss.

When he finally released her lips, she murmured, "You know, I'm not busy right now."

He laughed and pulled back slightly. "How about you introduce me to your friends first? Then I'll feed you."

"You don't have to do that."

"What? Meet your friends?"

"I want you to meet my friends, but you don't have to feed me since you cooked for me all week."

Sutton traced the bottom edge of her lower lip with his thumb. "I've liked having you around this week, London. More than I thought I would." After another kiss, he stepped back only far enough to drape his left arm over her shoulder.

They started toward Mel and Lelo. Mel wore a look of shock only less obvious than Lelo's.

"Did you tell your friends about me?" he asked softly.

"Just that I'd met a hot man. I didn't give them your name in case you didn't show up and I'd have to find me a new guy on the fly."

His arm fell away briefly so he could slap her ass. He grinned when she yelped. Then he whispered, "Oh ye of little faith. 'Fraid I'll have to punish you for that lapse."

"A hot lashing with your tongue or a spanking? Luckily, I'm good with either."

He nipped her earlobe. "Good to know. But it's not like I'm gonna let you choose which one *I* prefer."

"Funny."

"I wasn't joking. Now that you've shared your rope fantasy, I'll add it to mine that involves…you'll just have to wait and see, won't you?"

Holy. Hell. Heat licked the inside of her thighs.

Mel and Lelo stood side by side in front of Plato. Before London could offer introductions, Lelo blurted out, "Man-oh-man, you're Sutton Grant."

Sutton extended his hand. "Yes, I am. Who're you?"

"Lee Lorvin, but everyone calls me Lelo. It's so great to meet you. I'm a huge fan."

"Thanks."

Lelo stared and just kept pumping Sutton's hand until Mel shouldered him aside.

"Hiya handsome," she cooed. "I'm Mel Lockhart, London's fellow road dog. I too am a huge fan. I watched you win the CRA championship in Vegas the year Tanna Barker also won for barrel racing."

"Nice to meet you, Mel. Glad you were entertained that year."

"Uh, *yeah*, hard not to be jumping up and down outta my seat when you set the record for the fastest time."

London glanced at him, and the man seemed embarrassed by the focus on him. And she wanted to rub Mel's face in the dirt to see if that'd erase her expression of lust.

"So you're a barrel racer?" he asked Mel.

"No. I'm in the cutting horse division. Not as glamorous as the rodeo events people pay to see, but I do well."

"Bein' able to cut cattle out of a large herd is far more challenging and entertaining than any scheduled rodeo event," Sutton said. "It's a real skill that's needed in ranching."

London inwardly sighed at Sutton's sweetness in making sure Mel knew her competitive event was appreciated. What kind of man did that?

"Are you about healed up and ready to get back to competing?" Lelo blurted out, interrupting the conversation.

She felt Sutton stiffen beside her, but outwardly he stayed cool. "I'm in the 'wait and see' stage right now." He turned and kissed London's temple. "Luckily, I sweet talked London into working with my horse again while I'm at loose ends."

"That's right," Mel said. "I remember Berlin told me that London initially trained your horse at Grade A Farms."

"I knew she was the only woman for the job. I just had to convince her to take me on."

"You do have some interesting methods of persuasion, bulldogger."

He laughed. "You're gonna give your friends the wrong impression of me, darlin'."

"Not me," Mel quipped, "because I'm sure hoping you've got a dirty-minded, sweet-talking single brother."

"I've got two."

Mel's lashes fluttered. "They as big and good-looking and charming as you?"

"Mel!" London said with fake admonishment.

"What? It can't hurt to ask." She scooted closer to London to whisper, "You decide to get laid and the next thing I know you've hooked up with the smokin' hottie known as 'The Saint?' Girlfriend, I'm so proud of you I might just bust a button."

Lelo made a noise and they realized he was still staring slack-jawed at Sutton.

"Lelo, you're gonna catch flies if you don't shut your big trap," Mel drawled.

"Sorry. It's just...Sutton Grant. Your runs are damn near perfect. That's why folks call you 'The Saint' because you never screw up."

"Oh, I wouldn't say never. And that's not the only reason I've been called that." He sent London a conspiratorial wink. "But it doesn't apply this week, does it darlin'?"

"Stitch is gonna flip his shit when he meets you."

Ooh, mean-girl London clawed her way to the surface. "Pity then that I'm not invited to Stitch and Paige's party, isn't it?"

Lelo's mouth opened. Closed. Opened again. Then he cleared his throat. "Uh, well, maybe I spoke outta turn. I'm sure Stitch don't have no hard feelin's if you don't, London."

Sutton sent her an amused look. "Up to you darlin', what we do tonight. You know if I had my way we'd head to the camper right now and wouldn't leave until..." His heated head to toe perusal was as powerful as an actual caress. "Until tomorrow. Late tomorrow."

"Looks like you're shit outta luck, Lelo," London said breezily, laughing as Sutton started pulling her away.

Behind Lelo's back, Mel mouthed, "Call me you lucky bitch."

"You know where we'll all be if you change your mind," Lelo shouted after them.

* * * *

"That was fun."

Sutton draped his arm over her shoulder. "How far's your camper?"

She hip-checked him. "Friends first, then food, remember?"

"Right. And I'll bet we aren't skipping Stitch's party?"

"You bet your sexy ass we're not. It's not like we have to stay long, but you do need to put in an appearance for your adoring fans."

"And rub it in Stitch's face that you're no longer pining after him and you've moved on with me?"

London stopped, forcing Sutton to stop.

He faced her. "What?"

"I don't want you to get the wrong impression, Sutton."

"I'm not."

"Are you sure?"

"I don't know darlin', maybe you'd better spell it out for me."

London inhaled a fortifying breath and let it out. "About this deal. After seeing Lelo's reaction to you—to us—I'm glad that other people who've been looking at me with pity will be looking at me in a completely different light when they see us together."

"But?"

She inched closer and twisted her hand in the front of his shirt. "But my reason for wanting you to fuck me until I can't walk isn't for anyone's benefit but mine."

"And mine," he said softly. His eyes searched hers. "So I didn't misread the situation?"

"That what's been happening between us in private the past six days is only to make us look like a real couple in public?"

"Yeah."

"Until I saw you today, I wasn't sure. No, that's not true. I wasn't sure until after you kissed me and told me you'd had to go away because you couldn't *stay* away from me. That's when I knew there's nothing fake about the heat between us."

Sutton curled his hand around the side of her face and gave her a considering look.

"What?"

"You have good insurance on that camper? Because we're gonna set the inside on fire tonight."

The inferno in his eyes nearly torched her clothes. Right there in front of the white tent proclaiming "Jesus Saves." Tempting to shout, "Can I get an amen?!" and then crack jokes about her burning bush.

Instead she slipped her arm around Sutton's waist and pecked those delectable dimples. "Feed me first, bulldogger, then we'll get naked and test the combustible point of the mattress."

Chapter Eight

Sutton couldn't take his eyes off London. He'd catch himself staring at her mouth or those long, reddish-brown curls, or the flex of the muscles in her arm even when she just lifted her fork to eat.

She'd catch him gawking and as a reward, or hell, maybe it was punishment, she'd eye fuck him and run her tongue around her straw until his cock swelled against his zipper.

He leaned forward and grabbed her hand, bringing her knuckles to his mouth for a soft kiss. "You really think we'll make it through the party and the dance?"

"Who said I wanted to go to the dance?"

"You did. Last weekend. You said you always go."

"To the Saturday night dances. It's Friday night."

He raised his hand to the waitress. "Check, please."

London laughed. "Down boy."

"Been a while for me, darlin', and I'll need a round or five to build up my stamina."

"Don't scare me. I do have to climb on a horse the next two afternoons."

"Too bad for you. I plan on making you plenty saddle sore." He smirked. "I'm looking forward to kissing it and making it all better."

She turned her hand, threading their fingers together. "We need to get our minds off sex at least for a little while. Tell me something about you that's surprising."

Besides that I've been cleared to ride and I've been lying to everyone the past four months?

"No pressure. I'll rephrase. I'll go first. I've never been pierced. Your turn."

"Okay. I don't have any ink tattoos."

"But you've had a few rodeo tattoos."

"Yep. Your turn."

"I don't like anything butterscotch flavored."

"I do. Bring on the flavored body paint, baby. I'll lick you clean."

She groaned. "You are killing me. This was supposed to take our minds off sex."

"Darlin', I can't look at you and not think about all the ways I want to make you come. And if you'd prefer that I smear the body paint on your nipples or between your thighs?"

"Both." Her eyes heated. "I'm guessing the application would be as pulse-poundingly erotic as the removal."

"No reason to rush a good thing." He nibbled on the inside of her wrist. "It's your turn."

"My brain is stuck on whether I'd finally start liking the taste of butterscotch if I sucked it off your tongue after you licked it off me."

"Let's test that theory."

"Now?"

"I saw a bottle of butterscotch syrup at the ice cream place. I'll distract them. You swipe it and shove it in your purse."

"'The Saint' contemplating a heist for a dirty sexual scenario? I'm shocked. And more than a little turned on."

"Excuse me. Are you Sutton Grant?"

His gaze reluctantly moved from London's molten bedroom eyes to the guy standing at the end of the table. "That's me."

"I thought so, but I knew you were on the injured list for this season, so I was surprised to see you. Especially here at such a small-potatoes rodeo." He paused. "Are you competing?"

"Nope. I'm here with my girlfriend." He angled his head at London. "She runs a horse clinic."

The guy glanced over at London, and she gave him a finger wave.

"Oh. Wow. Sorry. Didn't mean to interrupt," he said with zero sincerity. "But as long as I'm here, can I get you to sign this?" He shoved a piece of paper at Sutton.

"Sure. What's your name?" Sutton made small talk as he scrawled his name and the date across the program. As soon as he finished, he saw there were several more people who'd lined up. He smiled and kept signing. This was part of the gig for a man in his position, with four championship buckles—the very buckle most of these guys would give their left nut to have a shot at.

After they were alone, he stood and threw some bills on the table. Then he offered London his hand. "Come on."

It'd gotten completely dark. The musical and mechanical sounds from the midway echoed with distortion and the bright lights sent the entire area aglow. "You wanna hit some of the rides before we crash the party?" He swung their joined hands. "Might be romantic to grope each other at the top of the Ferris wheel."

"Not romantic at all because I am a puker. No spinning rides for me."

"Poor deprived girl," he whispered. Then he tugged her into a darkened corner between two storage sheds, pushing her up against a modular home. "How about if I try and get that pretty head of yours spinning another way." Sutton kissed her, starting the kiss out at full throttle. Not easing up until she bumped her hips into his, seeking more contact.

God, she made him hard. He'd never wanted a woman this much, this soon. What sparked between them might be fueled by lust but it also went beyond it—which is what'd sent him running.

For now, he'd focus on that lust.

His hands squeezed her hips and then moved north to her breasts. He broke his lips free from hers and dragged an openmouthed kiss down her throat. When the collar of her shirt kept him from sampling more of her skin, he tugged until the metal snaps popped.

No bra. Nothing to get in the way of taking every bit of that sweet flesh into his mouth to be sucked and licked and tasted.

Her breath stuttered when his teeth enclosed her nipple. She knocked his hat to the ground as she clutched the back of his neck, pressing his mouth deeper against her.

Sutton shoved his thigh between hers. Immediately she rocked her hips against that hard muscle.

"Yes. Right there."

He lost track of all sanity as he nuzzled and suckled her sweet tits, stopping himself from jamming his hand down her pants and feeling her hot and creamy core as he got her off with his fingers. Choosing instead to get her off this way, because fuck, there was something primal about making her come nearly fully clothed.

"Harder."

London's head fell back against the building and she softly gasped his name as he gave her what she needed.

She'd clamped her thighs around his leg so tightly he felt the contractions in her cunt pulsing against his quad. He felt the matching pulse beneath his lips as he drew on that taut nipple. Felt her short nails digging into the back of his neck.

Fucking hell this woman tripped all his wires.

When she loosened her grip on him, he planted kisses up her chest, letting his breath drift along her collarbone, smiling when gooseflesh broke out beneath his questing lips.

"You are no saint, Sutton Grant."

"Nope." He nuzzled the curve of her throat.

"Mmm. Keep kissing me like that while I fix my shirt."

"I'm happy you didn't wear a bra."

"No need for me to wear one, well, probably ever."

"Lucky me."

She rubbed her lips across his ear, raising chills across his skin. "Brace your hands on the building by my head."

"Why?"

She nipped his earlobe. "Because I wanna kiss you."

As soon as he complied, he angled his head so she could better reach his lips.

But London dropped to her knees and started working on his belt.

"Sweet Christ, woman. What are you doin'?"

"Giving you a kiss."

"My mouth is up here."

"That's not where I wanna kiss you."

Any blood left in his head surged to his groin. The one teeny part of his brain that wasn't giving him mental high-fives managed to eke out, "What if someone comes up behind us?"

"You really care about that?" *Pop* went the button on his Wranglers. *Zip* went his zipper. She pulled back the jeans and shifted his boxer-briefs so his dick slid through the opening.

"Fuck, not really. Just giving you an out—holy fucking hell," he said when her hot mouth closed around his cock.

When she eased back and off him, he actually whimpered.

"Oh, bulldogger, you're just big all over, aren't you?"

Before he formed a coherent sentence, she sucked him to the root.

Again.

And again.

And again.

His body throbbed with the need for release. God. It'd been so long.

"London," he managed, "I'm about to..." That warning tingle in his balls lasted barely a blip before his cock spasmed and unloaded. Each hot spurt jerked his shaft into her teeth.

Her mouth worked him until he was utterly spent. He started to feel lightheaded, realizing he'd held his breath. After gulping in oxygen, the fuzzy sensation faded, but he still felt rocked to his core.

Then London was in his face. "Sutton, you'd better do up your jeans."

"Sure." Still in a daze, he pushed off the building. He kept his gaze on hers as he tucked in, zipped up, and buckled. Then he leaned in and kissed her. "Thanks."

"My pleasure."

"Fair is fair though, darlin'."

Her eyes widened. "What do you mean?"

"I wanna taste you. Undo your jeans."

"Sutton—"

"Now."

London's obedience surprised him as well as pleased him. Excitement tinged with fear danced in her eyes as she loosened her belt and unzipped, peeling the denim back. "I don't think—"

He slammed his mouth down on hers. Kissing her with a teasing glide of his tongue and soft licks, he pressed his palm over her belly, slowly sliding his hand over the rise of her mound and into her panties. When his middle finger breached the slick heat of her sex, he smiled, breaking their kiss. "You're wet," he said, his breath on her lips.

"Yes."

"It's so fucking hot that you're wet after blowing me." He followed the slit down to her center where all the sweetness pooled. After swirling his fingertips through her cream, he worked his hand out. Then he pushed back so only a few inches separated their faces and brought his hand up, letting her see the wetness glistening there, hyperaware they were close enough she could smell her own arousal.

Sutton slipped his fingers into his mouth and sucked the sweet juices, briefly closing his eyes to savor this first taste of her.

Before he completely pulled his fingers free, London was right there. Licking his fingers, tasting herself on him, sucking on his tongue. The kiss could've soared past the combustible stage, then neither of them would've been able to stop. But something made him hold back, turn the kiss into a promise of more to come as he dialed down the urgency. Easing back, he let his hands wander, wanting all of her but willing to wait until he could have her the way he needed.

London sensed the shift too. She fastened her jeans and fixed her belt. Her gaze finally hooked his, but he couldn't read her.

He traced the edge of her jaw. "What?"

"You pack a powerful punch, Sutton Grant."

"Same could be said about you, Miz Gradsky." Knowing they needed a break from the intensity, he reached down and grabbed his hat and settled it on his head. "You still wanna hit the party?"

"Of course. Now we've got a really good excuse for being fashionably late."

"So if someone asks where we've been?"

"I'll say we were messing around and lost track of time." She smoothed her hands over her hair and straightened her clothes. "It's the truth."

They returned to tent city hand in hand. The party wasn't hard to find.

Several guys stopped London to chat, and he had a surge of jealousy even when she introduced him right away. But they both discovered it wasn't necessary since he knew a lot of the people hanging around. Except the kids in line for the keg all looked younger than eighteen. Seemed like so long ago that he'd been the new kid on the circuit. Back then, seeing guys who were the age he was now had seemed so ancient.

Finally, they reached the spot by the fire where the couple hosting the party held court.

Sutton had only seen the pair last week from a distance. Stitch was a substantial guy—although Sutton had him by a couple inches—and he appeared to be four or five years younger than London, which is why Sutton didn't do a double take at seeing his baby-faced girlfriend. She was cute, miniature in stature. But her blonde hair, as big as the state of Texas—a phrase his friend Tanna used to say—added some height. He wondered if someone had warned the young thang about the perils of standing too close to the fire doused with that much hairspray. Or about the fuse-like dangers of the synthetic beauty queen sash she wore loosely draped across her chest.

Besides, Sutton was way more interested in this Stitch guy, the douche-nozzle dumb enough to dump long, lean London for pint-sized Paige.

Like most bulldoggers, Stitch was solid, but he'd gone a step further, bulking up to the point he'd lost his neck. Nothing else about him seemed remarkable, save for the fact the guy was bow-legged. Probably made Sutton an ass to wish the dude was cross-eyed, with buck teeth and nearly bald beneath his cowboy hat too, but there it was. Sometimes he wasn't a nice guy.

London's hand tightened in his. "Sutton."

"What?"

"Stop growling."

"Sorry." *Not at fucking all.* "Just feeling a little territorial, darlin'."

"I can see that. So can everyone else."

"Good."

Lelo elbowed Stitch and his entire body stiffened.

Then Stitch dropped his arm from Paige's shoulder and skirted the fire pit, heading toward them. He offered his hand first and Sutton automatically followed suit. "I can't believe *the* Sutton Grant is here at my campsite. I can't believe I'm meeting you. Man, I'm such a huge fan! Your run in Vegas was legendary. It was a dream to get to watch history being made."

"I appreciate you saying so."

"When Lelo said you were here, I thought he was pulling my leg. He's such a prankster."

"Maybe *his* name oughta be Stitch," Sutton deadpanned.

Stitch's eyes clouded for a second. He didn't get the joke.

Sutton kept his expression cool. As much as he appreciated Stitch's enthusiasm, it bothered the crap out of him that neither the man nor his girlfriend had acknowledged London.

Paige pushed her way between them and offered her hand, while keeping a proprietary hand on Stitch. "Hi. I'm Paige. We're happy you could stop by our party."

"We appreciate the invite."

Paige glanced at London, then refocused on Sutton. "I'm sure London has told you all about us, but we had no idea she'd met someone new."

Sutton smiled at London. "Don't know where you got the impression that London and I just met. I've known her for three years. We reconnected when I asked her to work with my horse, since she'd trained him at Grade A Farms." He brought their joined hands up and kissed the back of her hand. "And what a reconnection it's been."

London let her secret smile speak for her.

"Good to see you, London," Stitch said politely. "You're looking well."

"Thanks, Stitch."

Then Stitch launched into a barrage of questions that normally would've amused Sutton, but he was just so damn distracted by the woman by his side. The scent of her. The tiny taste of her still lingering on his tongue. The bonfire had nothing on the heat that rolled off her body. Then she started feathering her thumb across the inside of his wrist. Back and forth. Pressing into the vein to feel his pulse, teasing the sensitive spots as if it was his cock.

Enough. He wanted the real thing.

When Stitch took a breath, Sutton bent his head to whisper. "Let's go."

"We haven't been here ten minutes."

"I can be inside you in under ten minutes," he countered with a silken growl.

"We just wanted to drop in and say thanks for the party invite," London announced to Stitch and Paige, "but we've gotta get."

Sutton didn't bother masking his grin.

"But you just got here!" Stitch protested. "You haven't even had a beer yet."

"Thanks for your hospitality, but maybe next time. Nice meeting you."

"Maybe we'll see you at the fireworks?" Stitch said hopefully.

Sutton glanced into London's heavy-lidded eyes. "We'll be far too busy making our own fireworks to care about someone else's, won't we darlin'?"

"Yeah, baby, we will." She reached up and touched his cheek. "I missed you last night."

Looking into her eyes, Sutton knew none of this was for show—this moment, although played out in front of dozens—belonged only to them. "Same here. Let's go."

Chapter Nine

London felt Sutton's hot breath on the back of her neck as she fumbled with the key to unlock the camper. She closed her eyes, trying to calm down because this was it, this was where all the sexual teasing and banter had led to...being naked with Sutton Grant.

Holy fucking shit was she ready for this?

"London?"

"I'm sorry. I'm shaking so hard I can't get the key in the lock."

"Let me." He didn't grab the key, he just curled his body around hers, steadying her, making his hand an extension of hers. Metal clicked and the door popped open. He pressed a kiss below her ear and murmured, "After you."

She shuddered at the deep timbre of his rough and sexy voice.

"Should I be concerned about your hesitation?"

"No. Just stop whispering in my ear. It's distracting me."

"Mmm. Sweet thang, I'm gonna have so much fun telling you every dirty little thing I plan to do to you." He made a half growl against the side of her throat. "Then doing it." He sank his teeth into her skin and growled again. "At least twice."

That prompted her to take that first step inside. The door slammed behind them.

Sutton kept his hands on her shoulders as she led him to the bedroom. She'd cleaned off her bed but it hadn't improved the area much. Suddenly, she worried this might not be the best idea.

Then that liquid sex voice melted into her ear again. "Stop."

"What?"

"Whatever negative thoughts that're keeping us from climbing in that bed and crawling all over each other." He pressed his hips into her backside.

He tilted her head to the right and moved his hands over her collarbones to the front of her blouse and popped the buttons. One. At. A. Time.

As soon as he'd undone the last button, he slowly turned her to face him.

Keeping her eyes focused on her task, she undressed him in the same leisurely manner, enjoying the feel of his hot skin and contours of his muscles beneath her hands. All she could think about was feeling the press of his weight against her, feeling the musculature in his back with her fingers as he moved above her.

"You're killing me with that look in your eyes, London."

"The look that makes it very clear I want to lick you up one side and down the other?" She angled her head, breathing on the tight tip of his nipple before her lips circled it.

"Ah, Christ."

"You like that."

"Mmm. I'd really like it if we could speed things up." His hands followed the contours of her sides to the curve of her hips.

"What's the rush?"

"You," he whispered across her bared shoulder. "I wanna feel you—all of you—around me. Been wanting that for days."

That's when Sutton took matters into his own hands. He stepped back far enough that she could see him yank off his boots and socks. Then he unbuckled his belt and unzipped his jeans. He lifted one, sexy dark eyebrow, silently asking why she wasn't stripping.

London had an overwhelming rush of shyness. It was one thing to want him so desperately, to want to rip off his clothes and feast on him, to get lost in passion, to reach for each other in a haze of lust...so how had they gone from that to...this? Lowering her chin, she allowed her hair to fall over her face.

Rough-skinned hands cupped her shoulders. Then his fingers were beneath her chin and his avid mouth landed on hers, reigniting that passion. He kissed her with authority and greed while he stripped her out of her remaining clothes. His hands were everywhere, pinching her nipples, squeezing her hips, clamping onto her ass. They fell back onto the bed with Sutton on the bottom, breaking their fall.

His cock had gotten trapped between their bodies. Raising herself up on all fours, she automatically started rocking against it, kissing him frantically as the tips of her breasts rubbed against the hair on his chest.

Two sharp slaps on her ass burned like hell—but it caught her attention. She gasped, "What—"

"Scoot up."

Confused by another abrupt halt to their intimacy, her eyes met his. "Why?"

"I want your pussy on my face."

She blushed.

"London," he said with a sharper tone than she'd ever heard from him, "get on up here girl, before I smack that fine ass of yours again."

"B-but I've never—"

"Don't care. That little taste of you wasn't near enough." He held onto her inner thighs, pulling her up his body while he pushed himself down the bed. He slid his hands around to her butt cheeks and pressed her mound against his mouth.

Any thoughts London had about awkwardness vanished the instant that tongue came out.

A relentless tongue that licked her up one side and down the other. Probing her folds. Swirling inside the opening to her sex and then plunging deep. Teasing her clit with alternating soft flicks and licks.

His hands were hard, his fingers digging into her skin. The wet lapping noises of his mouth on her sex mixed with her soft moans and echoed in the tiny space.

Sutton pulled back to kiss the inside of her thigh. Then he nipped it hard and she cried out. It startled her more than hurt her, but even the tiny sting sent a shot of heat through her.

He made that sexy growling noise against the stinging spot. "Shoulda known a tough woman like you would like a little rougher play." Then he nipped the other thigh a bit harder.

London's gasp turned into a groan when he settled his hot, sucking mouth over her clit.

It'd been so long and he was so freakin' good with that naughty mouth of his. The tingling sensation immediately radiated down her spine, sending every hair from the back of her neck to her tailbone on full alert.

She threw her head back and said, "Oh-god-oh-god-oh-god don't stop! Please. That's so..." The orgasm hit—then it expanded and exploded. Each hard contraction had her knees quaking and her arms shaking.

When she opened her eyes, she realized she'd lowered herself completely onto Sutton's face and was probably smothering him. She tried to scramble back. "I'm sorry—"

Another hard whap landed on her butt and he scooted out from beneath her to stand at the end of the bed. "Never apologize for coming like that. Sweet heaven that was so damn sexy."

Next thing she knew he'd caged that big, strong body around hers. She arched into him. She might've purred.

Sutton's lips skimmed her earlobe. "I want you." His hot breath burrowed inside her ear. "Want you like fuckin' crazy." Then the tip of his tongue traced the shell of her ear. "Want you hard and fast this time." He kissed the hollow below her ear and her pulse skyrocketed. "Next go will be slow, sweet, and sweaty, okay?"

"Okay, yes, please."

He pushed back and she heard the crinkle of a condom wrapper. Then his knees moved between hers and work-roughened hands traveled the back of her thighs, stopping to tilt her ass to a better—God, hopefully deeper— angle. The tip traced her slit once before he wedged his cock inside her fully in a steady glide.

She'd held her breath, waiting for a hard thrust. So when Sutton layered his body over hers, all heat and muscle and strength, the air left her lungs in a long groan. He nudged aside her hair and planted openmouthed kisses from the nape of her neck to the ball of her shoulder and back.

Gooseflesh rippled across her body.

"You're so sexy, London. You drive me out of my ever-lovin' mind." Sutton curled his hands around her hipbones and pulled himself upright. His slow withdrawal lasted two strokes before he was ramming into her.

As much as she'd envisioned their first time together being face to face with their mouths fused and their hearts racing in unison as he rolled his body over hers, this was better. More intense. She rocked back into him. The slap of skin on skin and the rhythmic squeak of the bed created a sexual cadence that had her clenching around his pistoning shaft. Each time she bore down he'd make a deep, sexy noise of masculine satisfaction.

After about the fifth time, he said, "London. I can't hold off."

"Just a couple more. Please, I'm so close again."

Sutton quit moving, but he stayed buried balls deep inside her. He leaned over and murmured, "I'll getcha there. Squeeze me hard, baby. Really hard."

As soon as she released her tightened pussy muscles, his hand cracked on her butt and her cunt spasmed on its own.

She cried out, not in pain, but because that extra stimulation shoved her closer to the edge.

"Beautiful. Again."

London did that four more times, bore down, then felt the heat of Sutton's hand as she let go of her clenched inner muscles. Her body took over and she started to come wildly. The orgasm radiated out from her core, electrifying every inch of flesh. Every nerve ending flared to life.

That's when Sutton moved, plunging into her in the same tempo as the blood throbbing in her sex. Once her peak waned, he ramped up his pace, holding her steady as he shouted his release. Such a rush, feeling his big body shuddering behind her and the hard jerk of his shaft against her swollen pussy walls.

Then he went completely still.

Once he'd caught his breath, he caged her body beneath his again, pressing his chest against her from shoulders to hips. He nuzzled the back of her head and expelled a sigh. "You okay?"

"Way, way, way better than okay, Sutton."

"Me too. Lemme ditch the condom. Be right back." He kissed her again and withdrew.

She withheld a hiss, but her arms gave out and she collapsed on the bed.

Gentle hands turned her over and two hundred plus pounds of hot, hunky cowboy loomed over her. His kiss was so sweet and packed with such gratitude that she couldn't help but reach for him, twining her fingers in his thick hair. Running her palm down his spine and getting a handful of his muscled ass.

This man was full of surprises. Over the past week she'd learned to appreciate his quiet sense of humor, as well as his stillness. He was thoughtful and deliberate—such a welcome change from the rash and selfish assholes she'd dated in the past. He listened instead of jabbering on, but he could knock her down a peg if she needed it. He had a protective streak and yet he could soothe her with a simple touch. He loved animals. He was close to his family.

All those things would be more than enough to capture her interest. But add in his stunning good looks—although he tried to downplay them—his holy fuck body, and now learning he had a raunchy, bossy side behind the bedroom door, and she'd lost any hope of not falling madly in love with Sutton Grant.

Love. Jesus. What was wrong with her? No one falls in real true love in six days.

So this overwhelming sensation of satisfaction and excitement had to be a lust high, the happy discovery of sexual compatibility...not the kind of life-affirming love she wanted.

True to his intuitive nature, Sutton immediately sensed the change in her mood. He didn't do anything by half-measures. She should've recognized that right away. While that trait usually had her running the opposite direction, now she clung to it and to him.

"London. Sweetheart. What's wrong?"

Tell him.

Don't be an idiot.

She squeezed him more tightly. "I like being with you like this. And I'm kicking myself we haven't been doing this at every possible opportunity all week."

Soft lips brushed her forehead. "I was thinking the exact same thing."

"Oh yeah? What else were you thinking?"

He rolled them until she was on top, straddling his groin. His hand grabbed a fistful of hair and he tugged her head back, baring her throat. "I'm thinking I watched you riding my horse this week—and I've never been so jealous of a horse in my life. So after I get a chance to taste these sweet tits, I'll wanna see how well you ride me."

"That right?"

"Mmm-hmm. And baby, if you're really good, next time you can be guaranteed I'll wanna try out that riding crop on you."

Chapter Ten

Sutton towel dried his hair and watched London sleeping. Not a graceful sleeper. She was a sprawler. And she hadn't lied about being a snorer. She'd twisted the sheets into a knot, exposing her bare leg, allowing him to see the love bruises he'd sucked on the inside of her thighs. Damn if those red and purple marks didn't look sexy against her pale skin. Before they'd called it a night, he'd checked her ass to see if he'd left marks there from the whacks he'd given her. But he'd just found a few reddened hot spots and thumb and finger shaped bruises on her hips, cheeks, and the backs of her thighs.

A wave of want rolled over him, staring at the beautiful siren he'd worn out last night and who'd wrung him out. He'd never been fully able to explore his kink with any woman, besides a few slaps on the ass here and there—rarely during sex—and some limited rope play, one hand tied to the bed sort of thing. But London wanted more.

And heaven help him he wanted more too, and couldn't wait to see where the need for more would lead them.

Her arms moved overhead in a long morning stretch. She sighed softly and opened her eyes, zeroing in on him first thing. She smiled. "Hey, handsome."

"Hey yourself, gorgeous."

"How long have you been standing there watching me sleep? Because if I'm drooling, I swear it's a new thing since I finally had a drool-worthy man in my bed last night."

Sutton returned her smile. "I've been up fifteen minutes. Took a quick shower. I've been watching you because it's so fucking hot how you just give yourself over in bed whether you're asleep or awake."

London glanced away.

"Did I say something wrong?"

"No. You said something exactly right." Her hazel eyes were alight with happiness when she looked at him. "Last night was amazing. Beyond anything I ever imagined. But what I always wanted. I wasn't sure how you'd react this morning. Make sense?"

"Perfect sense. It's that way for me too. That's why I've been standing here watching you."

"Seriously?"

"Yeah."

She brushed her hair from her face but didn't attempt to cover up her breasts as she waited for further explanation.

But Sutton was done talking. For now. "I imagine you want coffee?"

"Mmm. A man who will spank me during sex, make me coffee the next morning, and looks that damn good in a floral towel?" She sighed gustily. "Score one for team Gradsky."

He laughed. "Coffee will be done by the time you get cleaned up."

While London took a quick shower, Sutton called Ramsey at the gun range and asked the sample tests be e-mailed to him right away so he could study for the range master test. If he failed, he was out nothing. After he hung up, he really wanted to share the possible change in his life with someone, but his excitement dimmed when he realized he couldn't tell anyone. Especially not London. Things were on an uphill swing with them— not just because they were burning up the sheets. And besides, she'd been working with Dial less than a week. Doubtful the horse had made great strides in such a short amount of time.

As soon as London stepped out of the back room, fully dressed, Sutton wrapped his arms around her. She melted into him, sharing the sweet type of morning kisses he craved. "You smell great and I know firsthand that you taste even better."

"Stop blocking my access to coffee."

They sat at the small table in the front, which he noticed for the first time had been completely cleared. "Where's all your jewelry stuff?"

London blinked at him as she gulped coffee.

"London?"

"It's around."

"Not around here. Where is it?"

"Don't get mad."

He fucking *hated* when women said that because it was guaranteed to blow his top. "Where is it?"

"You had way more room at your place and I knew you'd be staying here this weekend, and we needed the space, so I hoped it wouldn't be that big of a deal if I moved it into your house. Temporarily."

"Why would I be mad about that? You've already brought some of it in."

"I don't know. Most guys get weird about their latest squeeze infringing on their space."

"I'm not most guys, sweetheart." His gaze hooked hers, silently asking, *calling yourself my latest squeeze is insulting to both of us, doncha think?*

She turned away to pour herself another cup of coffee.

He let it go. "What's on the agenda today?"

London snagged a clipboard before she sat. "I'm booked solid but I did leave myself two hours for lunch."

"What did you and Stitch used to do during breaks?"

That surprised her—almost as if she'd forgotten about him. "We didn't get breaks at the same time very often. But he always wanted to wander through the crowds. See and be seen." She shrugged. "As long as I get fed, I don't care what we do."

"Need me to hang around the corral and help you out today?"

Another look of surprise. "Why would you wanna do that?"

"It's gotta beat sitting alone in the camper."

"Don't you want to go...?"

"To watch the rodeo contestants and stock contractors? Nope. To the midway? Nope. Go chat up all my great buddies still running the blacktop? Oh, right. Hanging with them guys never was my scene." Sutton leaned over and tugged on her ponytail. "Looks like you're stuck with me."

She smiled and stole a kiss. "Looks like. Let's hit it."

* * * *

It should've been boring, watching London working horses, conferring with young riders and their parents. But there was such enthusiasm surrounding her, as well as strength and confidence that he couldn't focus on anything else except her. Wanting her, needing her, taking her.

The instant her break started, he herded her toward the camper. She fumbled with the keys again, but in her defense he did have her body pressed up against the door leaving her little space to maneuver.

"Sutton. What are you doing?"

"I'm about to fuck you right here against your camper door in broad daylight if you don't get us inside."

"This door is flimsy. If you wanna fuck me hard, I'd suggest we hit the floor."

The door flew open. Somehow they managed to get it shut and locked before they were on each other.

And the floor held up just fine.

* * * *

Afterward, they strolled hand in hand through the exhibitors' hall. If Sutton would've had his way they would've spent the last hour of her break alone inside the camper. It bothered him that even after their intimate connection, which London admitted she'd never had with another lover, that she was still on the *look-at-my-new-man* kick with Stitch.

That's what you signed on for. Showing her you are the better man is the best way to combat any feelings she might still have for him.

London stopped at a jewelry stand. She chatted with the owner, asking about square footage rental charges, revenue, venue commission percentage kickbacks. All the while Sutton stayed so close behind her he could feel the rumble of her laughter vibrating against his chest.

Finally she said, "Thank you so much for your time."

As soon as they were out of earshot, Sutton said, "Do you know her?"

"No. But I'm interested in whether running a seasonal jewelry storefront is profitable."

"You thinking about starting one for the jewelry you've been making?"

London stopped and faced him. "Do you think it's a frivolous venture? A waste of my time and energy?"

He framed her face in his hands. "No. If you love making the jewelry you'll keep doin' it regardless if it's profitable. You're savvy enough to talk to the people in the trenches before you make any decisions. Sweetheart, that is just smart business. Anyone who tells you otherwise needs their head examined before getting their ass kicked."

"You are so..."

"What? Don't leave me hanging here."

"Surprising. You're smart, with the perfect mix of raunchy and sweet."

Sutton leaned forward to graze her lips, tasting her and breathing her in. "Will it scare you off if I admit I'm really crazy about you?"

"No. Will it scare you off if I say I really need you to kiss me right now like you are that crazy about me?"

"C'mere and gimme that mouth." He deepened the kiss, keeping the passion simmering below the surface.

She kissed him back with the single-minded absorption in the moment he'd come to expect from her. Everything but her faded away.

He had no idea how long they'd been lost in the kiss until he heard a throat clearing behind them.

Reluctantly releasing her lips, he let his hands fall way.

London opened her eyes and stared at him, equally dazed.

"No offense, but you two are kinda blocking the aisle."

Sutton looked over his shoulder and saw Stitch standing there, his hands in the front pockets of his jeans, his gaze on London.

His suspicions kicked in. Had London asked him to kiss her like that only because she'd seen Stitch?

Dammit. None of what'd been happening between them was playacting on his side. Was it on hers?

London wrapped her arm around Sutton's waist and they faced Stitch. "Oh, hey, sorry. We'll get out of the way."

"No, no that's okay. I had a few questions for Sutton anyway, if he's got time."

"Gosh, that'd be swell, but we were headed to the midway so I can win my lady a prize." Sutton leaned forward and confided, "London has this theory that faithful men are as mythical creatures as unicorns, so I'm gonna prove her wrong. And win her the biggest stuffed unicorn I can find as a daily reminder that I am the man she can count on."

Poor kid looked confused as hell.

Over the course of the weekend, Stitch wore that expression a lot.

Chapter Eleven

The second week that London shared Sutton's living space was markedly different than the first week.

They spent a large portion of their time naked—in every room in the house. London never knew what to expect from Sutton either in bed or out of it. The first afternoon back from the Henry County Fair, he'd borrowed one of his brother's horses so they could ride together. Which had been fun, even when she kept an eye on Sutton to make sure he didn't show off, act all macho and hurt himself—not that the man seemed injured at all. He was in better physical condition than any man she knew. It also meant that she'd met his brothers, who'd been equally shocked to meet her.

Then the following night he'd grilled steaks and they'd sat outside beneath the starry sky and had fallen asleep entwined together on his puffy outdoor chaise lounge.

The one night he'd left her alone because he had mysterious "other commitments" she found herself watching the clock as she crafted eight necklaces, anxious for him to come home. The man had been so impatient to have her he'd practically swept all her beads off the kitchen counter like in one of those romantic movies. But the way he'd fucked her on the counter had been hot and nasty—X-rated—not a romantic thing about it, thank god.

They'd watched TV together. Cooked together. Danced around the house and the patio in the moonlight together. They'd made love in every position imaginable. Sometimes their interludes included kink—London still remembered the high from when he used ice on her after he'd bound her hands and how he'd heated up all the cold spots with his hot mouth. Sometimes their interludes were just hot and fast—new lovers who couldn't keep their hands off each other. Sometimes Sutton woke her up in the middle of the night, loving on her with such tenderness she wondered if she'd dreamt it. Which was a real possibility because not one night in the last week had he spent the entire night in her bed.

London continued to work with Dial, but she'd cut the horse's training sessions short because there wasn't much more she could do with him. Not that she could tell Sutton that yet. Partly because just after two short weeks she wasn't ready to close the deal she'd made with him. For one thing, whenever she asked the bulldogger if he'd been cleared to compete, he changed the subject, so she knew he was hiding something. But what? Did it have anything to do with her?

The one wrinkle in their intimacy was Sutton hadn't invited London to move into his bedroom. If they made love in a bed, it was hers in the guestroom. Even if Sutton fell asleep with her afterward, when she woke in the middle of the night or at dawn, the man was gone. That didn't mean he'd just crashed in his bed. No. That meant gone—she couldn't find the man in his house.

She hadn't tried to track him down, figuring if he needed time alone outside or wherever, then it wasn't her place to disturb him.

In the last day he'd become restless, but in a brooding manner. London suspected mindless chattering would get on his nerves so she...did exactly that. Jabbered on and on until he'd threatened to gag her. She'd retorted if he gagged her, he'd better plan on spanking her too.

That's how she ended up gagged with her own thong, her hands roped up with pigging string, bent over the back of the couch as Sutton whacked her bare ass until she came. Twice. Then he replaced the gag with his cock and she'd sucked him off, loving the sharp sting as he pulled her hair, which countered the gentle caress of his thumb on her jaw as he released in her mouth.

Afterward, he'd carried her to her bed and spooned her. She'd soothed him, but he still wasn't quite himself.

Right before she dozed off, she murmured, "Sutton, baby, you know you can talk to me about anything."

"I know. I just...can't. Not yet."

When she'd awoken in the morning, Sutton was gone.

As the weekend loomed, she didn't give a damn if they ran into Stitch and Paige or not. After being with Sutton, she knew even if Stitch came crawling back on his hands and knees she wouldn't take him back. She didn't want him. Hell, she'd never wanted him like she wanted Sutton. So any time Sutton asked about a specific plan to make Stitch jealous, she changed the subject.

Tit for tat, my man. You tell me what you're hiding and I'll admit you ruined me for all other men and I'm milking the training in the hopes you'll fall for me as hard as I've fallen for you.

* * * *

These late nights were killing him.

Sutton had agreed to help out his family by haying the field closest to his house. Cutting and baling was tedious work and left him more tired than if he'd run a marathon.

But he couldn't say no to his brothers—they'd pulled his ass out of the fire plenty of times. He couldn't say no to London—being with her was always the high point of his day. So the only time he had to practice the shooting requirements was after normal people went to bed. Add in the practice written tests, which weren't as easy as Ramsey claimed, and he'd been skating by on two hours of sleep a night.

Since last weekend's county fair was only forty-five minutes from his place, London decided to make the drive to her clinics every day rather than stay overnight.

Sutton had breathed a huge sigh of relief because it gave him the extra time he needed to study and prepare for the range master test. It also indicated that London had moved on for real in the make-Stitch-jealous game.

They'd entered the third week of their deal, trade—whatever it was. If he could make it through the next ten days, he'd be golden. Hopefully he'd pass the test, then he could come clean to London and his family about his future career plans and settle into a real relationship with his hot-blooded horse trainer. She'd seemed a little distant the past couple of days.

He'd managed to get two hours of dead-to-the-world sleep. Upon waking, he crept into the guest bedroom, intent on putting his wide-awake state to good use—waking London up with his face between her thighs. Nothing revved his engines like sucking down her sweet juice first thing in the morning.

The first time she came, she'd arched so hard against his mouth that his teeth had pressed into her delicate tissues. The tiny bite of pain had her fingers gripping his hair as the orgasm pulsed through her. Then he'd instructed her to grab onto the headboard and hold on.

The wait for orgasm number two, when she couldn't direct him at all, was much longer. Sutton took his time exploring her reactions. Suckling just her pussy lips. Jamming his tongue into her hole. Lightly flicking the skin surrounding her swollen clit but avoiding direct contact with the pulsing bundle. Slipping two fingers into her wet cunt, he spread her open and feasted until she begged him to let her come. When he relented and focused entirely on her clit, London's body quivered and she'd screamed her release.

Her pussy walls were still pulsating when he rammed his cock in deep. He paused for a moment, watching the sunbeams fall across her face. Probably, he should've made love to her with a gentle wake up.

But Sutton was too far gone. "The Saint" that London teasingly called him was still sawing logs; his beast was ravenous for a hard morning fuck. The headboard banged into the wall as he relentlessly hammered into her, sweat dripping into his eyes, his jaw tightened in anticipation with every stroke into that tight, wet heat. His fingers curled over hers on the brass bars, the backs of her thighs pressed against his chest. Her calves on his shoulders provided extra resistance as he drove his cock into her over and over.

After he'd spent himself—physically and emotionally—he unhooked their hands from the headboard and placed a soft kiss on each of her anklebones, then slowly lowered her legs to the mattress. He planted more kisses up the center of her body. Looming over her, he pecked her once on the lips. "Good morning, beautiful."

"Helluva way to start the day, bulldogger," she said with a satisfied feminine sigh. Her fingertips scraped the stubble on his cheeks. "I like the way this feels on the inside of my thighs."

When she kept petting him but didn't speak, he said, "Something wrong?"

"No. I was just happily surprised to have you in my bed this morning."

Sutton suspected this question would come up. He wasn't sure how to answer it. "We shared a bed in the camper for two nights on two different weekends." And it'd killed his back.

"But we didn't get much sleep. Oh. Now I get it. That's why we're in separate bedrooms? So you're not tempted to fuck me all the time and we can rest between rounds to keep it hot and exciting?"

"Smartass."

Her eyes clouded. "Why don't you want to sleep in the same bed with me? Do I snore? Did I fart?"

"Why're you taking the blame?" He kissed the frown line between her eyes. "I don't wanna fight with you. It's not a big deal that our sleep patterns don't mesh."

London slid out from beneath him and perched on the edge of the bed. "You're right. It's not a big deal. And it won't matter tonight because I won't be here."

"What? Why not?"

She stood and slipped on her nightgown. "Commuting from here will work most days, just not today."

Sutton studied her. Something else was going on with her. "And tomorrow? Are you coming back here before we head to the Jackson County

Fair?"

London fiddled with the bow on her nightgown strap. "We'll see."

The idea of her not being here, not talking to her, not touching her, kicked him into sort of a red rage. She was not inserting herself into his life so completely, making him fall for her, and then just walking away, leaving him so crazy about her that he'd do anything to keep her.

Anything except telling her the truth.

He yanked his sweatpants on and pulled his T-shirt over his head. "We're not doin' this."

"Not doing what? Being honest with each other? You're the one who's keeping to himself. If I didn't know better, I'd think you were sneaking off and trying to rope and ride in the middle of the damn night. But since I haven't seen you out in the barn at all in the last weeks since I started working with Dial, I know that's not where you've been keeping yourself."

Sutton hesitated all of ten seconds. "You really wanna see what I've been up to and where I've been?"

"Yes!"

"It'll change things between us."

London cocked a hand on her hip. "Some things need to change between us, Sutton."

"Fine." He snagged her hand. "Don't say I didn't warn you."

They stopped in front of the door at the far end of the hall. He opened the little box next to the doorframe that looked like a thermostat and punched in a code. The locks disengaged and he turned the door handle.

"After you."

London said nothing as she ducked inside.

After the door shut and latched behind them, he flipped on the main lights and led her down the stairs, keeping his back to her.

The space had been completely finished. Textured walls, acoustic ceiling, tile flooring, a built-in gun vault, locking cabinets for ammo. Tall benches lined the walls with a pegboard between the bench and the cabinets. The corner held a reloading station.

Sutton loved the absolute silence in his hidey hole. Once that upper door closed, he was vacuum-sealed in. The apocalypse could happen above him and he'd be oblivious. For that reason, so he didn't venture into "survivalist" territory, he didn't keep so much as a can of soda down here, say nothing of cases of weanies and beans and plastic jugs of water.

The actual range had been built from huge circular sections of concrete culverts. The targeting system was on an electronic pulley that ran along the top and bottom, allowing him to change the size, angle, and the distance of the practice targets with the push of a button.

It'd been an unconventional choice, foregoing a traditional basement family room, but he never regretted creating this for himself.

"Omigod! What is this place?"

Sutton hated—*hated*—London's wide-eyed look of horror as her gaze encompassed the space, as if she expected to see electrical tape, mini-saws, an array of pliers, dental instruments, and other devices of torture. "It's a gun range."

"*Inside* your house?"

Technically it was under his house, but he said, "Yeah."

"You have a fucking *gun range* inside your house?" she repeated.

It wasn't like she hadn't been raised around guns—her dad was a huge gun collector. He'd even invited Chuck to come over and shoot. He forced himself to keep his tone cool. "So? Some people have photography studios or theater rooms or a woodworking shop." He shrugged. "Shooting is my hobby. So I had a regulation range put in."

"But...isn't that illegal?"

"Jesus, London. You think I'm the law-breaking type? You think I would've showed it to you if I was trying to keep it on the down low?"

"Don't get snappy with me. I didn't realize people could have a gun range inside their house!" she snapped back.

"It's not that uncommon," he assured her. "I had dozens of designs to choose from. I first got the idea when a guy on my college rodeo team showed me his dad's inside shooting range."

"I assume the guy lived in a rural area like this?"

Sutton shook his head. "In town. Don't know what the building code restrictions are there, I know I had to jump through some hoops here to get approval and to pass inspection afterward."

London marched up to him and jabbed her finger into his chest. "Why didn't you tell me about this?"

"Because—"

"This is where you've been disappearing to at night?"

"Mostly. Some nights I work out. And I didn't think it'd be in my best interest to tell my houseguest that I was down here target shooting while she slept."

Her eyes narrowed. "What if I would've stumbled down here in the middle of the night? Would you've shot me as an intruder?"

"For Christsake, London! I'm not a fucking trigger-happy rube! And you can't just *stumble* down here because the area is secured with a coded locking system and a self-closing door. That means even if you get pissed off, know the code and come down here looking for my Smith and Wesson .460 to do some real damage to me, unless you chop off my thumb to get biometric access to my gun vault, you ain't getting nothing but even more pissed off."

"Don't even joke about that."

"I'm not. And see that?" He pointed to the red ambulance light on the ceiling. "If someone opens the door while I'm down here, it triggers an alarm. I cannot be caught unaware." Then he pointed to the range itself. "That enclosed space is bulletproof. I can't shoot out, no one can shoot in. I also have a secret panic alarm that goes straight to the sheriff's department."

"God. It's like I'm in Dr. Evil's underground lair."

He clenched his jaw and bit out, "Dr. Evil? Seriously?"

"No. But goddammit, Sutton, you had to expect I'd be freaked out by this."

She had him there.

"This"—she gestured around the space without breaking eye contact with him—"is an important part of who you are, isn't it?"

"Yeah."

"Why didn't you tell me? Not just about the James Bond underground thingy, but that you—"

"Had something in my life besides bulldoggin'?"

"Yes."

Not accusatory or hurt, but more curious. So he really felt like a total fucking heel for keeping this from her, too. "Because shooting has always been just mine in a way that bulldoggin' never will be. I do it for enjoyment. It's the one thing that's kept me sane during this last recovery."

They were nose to nose, breathing hard, staring at one another.

"Are you a good shot?" she asked softly.

"Darlin', I put a gun range in my basement. What do you think?"

Then she took a step back and her gaze roamed over him, head to toe, the return journey much slower as she seemed to catalog every inch of him, as if she was seeing him for the first time. When their gazes met, something had changed in London's eyes.

"Jesus. What now?"

"Do you ever wear those special military clothes when you're down here shooting?"

He frowned. "You mean like camo?"

"No." Her eyes were firmly on his chest. "The kind of clothes that black ops guys wear. A tight black T-shirt and black cargo pants tucked into biker boots, and a belt with a place for your gun, ammo, and maybe a pair of handcuffs? Ooh, and those mysterious wraparound sunglasses."

Sutton watched as she bit her lip. Then it dawned on him. She was turned on by the idea of him packing heat.

His cock went as hard as steel.

This was a far better reaction than fear. And if she wanted to play gun range taskmaster and novice shooter? He'd give it a whirl.

"When's the last time you fired a gun?" he asked gruffly.

"It's been a long time. And I never was very good at it."

He crowded her. "We'll change that right now."

"What? I'm in my damn pajamas!"

"So? Gimme your hand."

"Sutton—"

"In here I'm the teacher, and darlin', you *don't* get to argue with me." He snatched her hand. "A Glock will be too big for you. Let's start out with a thirty-eight."

"Thirty-eight what? Shots?"

"Thirty-eight caliber." His eyes searched hers. "You really don't know anything about guns?"

"Besides they're loud and dangerous? No."

A slow grin spread across his face. "That's what makes them so fun."

Her palms slid up his chest. "So the question is you gonna show me how to handle your big gun?"

In that instant, Sutton knew total acceptance. He knew those voices in his head telling him what he felt for her had gone beyond just lust and amusement and straight to love hadn't been taunting him. Still, he kept his tone light. "The one I want you handling has some heft to it. It heats up real fast."

"Show me."

He bent down and brushed his lips across the top of her ear. "You will listen to me and do exactly as I say."

She swallowed hard. "Yes, sir."

"Feel free to look around while I get out the guns and ammo." Sutton opened the safe and removed one gun—a thirty-eight Ruger revolver. When he turned around, London was staring at him. "What?"

"You are the most fascinating man I've ever met. And I've just touched the tip of the iceberg with you. I wonder what other secrets are beneath the surface."

"It's always the quiet ones you have to worry about," he joked.

"Sutton. I'm serious."

"Me, too. Come on. Let's load and shoot." He unlocked the gun cabinet and took down the box of bullets. He flipped the cylinder out and shoved in six bullets. "This first round I'll have you watch. Then I'll get you situated to shoot." Sutton snagged his ear protection and the plastic eye protection from the pegboard. There were half a dozen other sets of ear and eye protection hanging there, and he handed her the smallest set. "You can stand behind me and watch. And pay attention, sweetheart, 'cause there's gonna be a test."

Sutton ducked into the shooting area and started the ventilation system. He chose a target, picked the range, and hit the button that sent it back to his coordinates. He moved his neck side to side, shrugged his shoulders, and dropped them down as he widened his stance. Once he'd picked up the gun, he inhaled a slow breath and released it before he fired. Six times. He punched the button and the target returned. He'd clustered his shots, pretty damn perfectly if he did say so himself. Practice was paying off for him. He faced her.

Crazy woman smiled and gave him a double thumbs-up.

After he left the shooting area, London said, "I know you want me to have a turn, but I'd really like to see you do that again."

"Fine. Let's reload. You're doing it this time. And be careful because the barrel is hot."

"Why don't you just take the box of ammo in with you?"

"It's a safety protocol. Don't reload where you shoot. Full clip going in, empty clip going out. I follow that even when I'm down here by myself."

"Such a rule follower you are, Mr. Grant."

"On most things? Yes." He let his hot gaze sweep over her sexy, pajama-clad form. "But I wanna break all the rules when it comes to you, darlin'."

Sutton shot another round. Then he brought London into the shooting area and did the clichéd instructor move where he stood behind her, his arms alongside hers as she pointed the gun. He adjusted her stance. He whispered instructions in her ear. She wasn't easily distracted, which was a good sign. But she was aware of his hard cock nestled against her ass as he maneuvered her into position.

Gun loaded, he stood behind her as she sited the target. She fired off all six shots in rapid succession. The target showed five hits, so one shot had gone wild.

"Let's go again. That's not bad."

By the sixth round, London had become more comfortable.

But Sutton's pleasure receptors had overloaded. He was in his gun range with a sexy woman who wore very few clothes and delighted in making "big gun" and "quick on the trigger" and "hot barrel" jokes while sending him—and his cock—smoldering looks. Add in the scent of gun smoke that hung in the air around them and the buzz in his ears from the gunfire, and he was in bad shape. He needed her right fucking now.

"Sutton? Are you okay?"

When his gaze collided with hers, she gasped. "Baby, let's do something about that. But you've gotta put away your toys first."

As soon as he'd locked away the revolver and box of bullets, he was on her. Kissing her desperately, fumbling with her clothes, needing her skin beneath his hands while his body covered hers. Owned hers.

Sutton took her down to the floor on her hands and knees on the rug in front of the lone easy chair, his cock, head, and heart pounding. The violent need for her had him hiking her hips in the air, pinning her shoulders down with one hand while the other guided his cock between her legs.

But something stopped him.

He glanced down at London, the sexpot who was always up for anything, and he knew she deserved better than this. She liked it as rough and raunchy as he did, but right now he wanted to give her more of himself. "London. Sweetheart. Turn over."

A haze of lust had already clouded her eyes. "What's wrong?"

"Nothing. I just wanna look into your eyes when I'm loving on you." He levered himself over her. Those muscular thighs of hers automatically circled his waist. He tilted her pelvis and pushed inside her slowly, feeling her snug pussy walls relax to let him in. His hand shook when he brushed her hair off her face. "You are so beautiful." He kissed her with awe. The gentle mating of their mouths sent warmth flowing through him. "Beautiful and sexy. Sweet and nasty. Is there a more perfect woman on the planet for me?"

"Sutton."

"I think not. I can say it, but I don't think you believe it. Let me show you."

He kissed and touched and tasted her, dragging out the pleasure until their bodies were both slick with sweat.

Her fingers dug into his ass and her back bowed off the floor when he kicked up the pace. "Please, I can't take any more, this is..."

"For me too. Move with me."

She did. They were in perfect synchronicity.

When he hit that tipping point and the first wave of pulsing heat erupted, he'd been tempted to close his eyes.

But London's whispered, "Look at me and let me see you let go," had him locking eyes with her.

It was one of the most startlingly intimate moments he'd ever experienced.

His entire being shook in the aftermath. He nuzzled and kissed her, needing that grounding contact with her warm skin. "Thank you," he murmured against her lips.

"Can we just stay like this for a little while?" London nibbled on his jawline. "I'm not ready to return to the real world yet."

"Of course." He rolled so she was on top, wishing he had a blanket to cover her.

After a bit, she said, "You know, these benches would be a great place for me to work on my jewelry."

"Yeah?"

"Yeah. Then sometimes I could be down here and keep you company while you're shooting."

"I'd like that." More than she knew.

Chapter Twelve

London glanced at her watch. Where was Sutton? He should've been here fifteen minutes ago.

The funnel cakes were tempting. Rather than give in to her desire for fried dough covered in powdered sugar, she wandered to the next vendor site. The tent blocked the heat of the day and a fan from the back blew the first cool air she'd felt since she'd sat in her truck this morning.

She stayed there, pretending to look at the racks of handmade jewelry.

A familiar voice said, "London?"

Don't turn around. Maybe he'll go away.

"Never thought you were into jewelry. I'da bought you stuff like this if I thought you'd wear it."

I didn't need you to buy me stuff like this. I made stuff like this, dipshit, or don't you remember?

"You got your earplugs in or something?" Stitch clapped her on the shoulder, forcing her to face him.

"Oh hey, Stitch. What are you doin' here?"

"Killin' time until tonight."

"Without Paige?" came out a little snotty.

"Yeah. I wanted to surprise her with a little something." He paused. "Probably be wrong of me to ask for your help, huh?"

Do you think, fuckwad?

London shocked even herself when she said, "She'd probably like anything with sparkles or rhinestones."

"Paige does like her pink stuff."

They stood side by side, looking at jewelry—for her ex-boyfriend's new girlfriend. Talk about bizarre. London spied a lapel pin with a rhinestone crown on it. Tacky, but perfect for a princess. "I think she'll dig this."

Stitch nodded. He fingered the points on the crown. "So you and Sutton Grant, huh?"

"Yep."

"He's a good guy."

"That he is."

"I've always admired him. A lot. I watch his performance tapes all the time. His runs are picture perfect." He chuckled. "Except for that one last year. I was happy to see he didn't have permanent injuries. Man, he wrecked bad. You normally only see that in rough stock events."

"Sutton is fortunate."

Silence stretched between them. Then Stitch blurted, "Dammit, London, I'm so sorry that things ended up the way they did between us."

She looked at him, half expecting to see him wringing his hat in his hands. His blue eyes were filled with wariness; his cheeks were red with embarrassment. That's when she remembered why she'd fallen for the cute cowboy in the first place. Stitch was a sweet guy. Their four-year age difference hadn't mattered to her, but now she realized they'd always been in different places in their lives. While she patted herself on the back for lighting a fire in his Wranglers, in truth she'd been more his teacher for sex and dealing with his horse than his girlfriend. As much as it pained her to admit it now, she understood why he'd wanted something different.

They'd had some good times together. But if she really thought hard about it, she'd always known in her heart that they weren't right for each other for the long haul.

So was she repeating the pattern with Sutton? Training his horse and having hot, kinky, wild sex with him?

No. There was an emotional connection she'd never had with a man before. And she suspected Sutton felt it too. But since she'd blurted out her love for Stitch within the first month, this time, when it mattered, she'd be more cautious.

"London?"

She realized she'd gotten lost in her thoughts. "Sorry. I just wish you'd talked to me instead of sending me a lousy text message. Was that your idea or Paige's?"

He blushed. "Mine. Paige knew I was with someone when she and I first started hanging out. When we realized we wanted to be more than friends...I just ended it right then so we could be."

"You didn't think I'd be upset? Or that I deserved an explanation?"

"What was I supposed to say? Especially since we'd spent more time apart than together those last couple months."

"Is that when you and Paige started seeing each other?"

"Yeah, but as friends. And just so you know, because we never talked about it, Paige and I didn't... I mean we weren't...We hadn't..." He blushed harder.

Good lord. How had she ever ended up naked with this guy? "You and Paige weren't bumping uglies while you were still with me?"

"No! I'd never do that." His fist closed around the piece of jewelry. "I liked you, London. A whole lot. But meeting Paige... I never felt anything like it. She's just the one. And she feels the same way about me." Stitch's blue eyes met hers. "This ain't a fling with her."

"Like it was with me."

He nodded.

Just then, something inside her shifted. If she had to lose out—although now she suspected it was just getting dumped that'd had her seeing red— she'd rather lose out to true love.

"So are you gonna be mad at me forever? Cause we'll be seeing each other for years yet if we're both working the circuit."

She grudgingly said, "No. But I'd be happy if you talked to Paige about keeping her animosity leashed. She doesn't have anything to worry about when it comes to me."

"I'll talk to her about backing off."

"That'd be good. I'm..." *Just say it.* "Happy for you finding the real deal."

"You are?" His eyes nearly bugged out of his head.

"Hard to believe, but yes. Because now, after being with Sutton for such a short time, I know it can happen."

Stitch grinned. "Cool." Then he pulled her into his arms for a hug. He whispered, "Thank you for the forgiveness, London. I never meant to hurt you."

"I get that now." Before she could step back, they were ripped apart.

An infuriated Sutton demanded, "What the fuck is this?"

"I, ah, well, London and I—"

"Tryin' to get back into her bed and into her life, weasel? Guess what? It ain't ever happening because I'm there now and I take up a lot of goddamned room, and I'm not goin' anywhere. *Ever.*"

"Sutton!"

He got right in Stitch's face. "Are you one of them guys who only wants what he can't have?"

Stitch stumbled back.

London could tell that Stitch's vocal cords had frozen in mortification from being dressed down and physically intimidated by his idol. So naturally she jumped in to protect him. "Leave him alone."

Sutton's gaze snapped to her. "Why are you defending him?"

"Because you are bein' an ass. And in public."

"Tell me I didn't just see this man with his arms around you."

"Oh, for Christsake."

"I saw it. I watched you and him all cozied up, chatting like it was old home week." He glared at Stitch. "Where's your girlfriend?"

"Uh, she and I—"

"Broke up?" Sutton supplied. "So that leaves you free to—"

London covered Sutton's mouth with her hand. "Shut your face before you say anything more ridiculous than you already have." When he tried to jerk away, she twisted the fingers of her other hand into his shirt and hissed, "Asshat." Then she looked over her shoulder at Stitch. "Sorry. I'm pretty sure he's been at the bar all afternoon."

"Oh. Well, then, I'm gonna git." He sent Sutton an odd look then threw his shoulders back. "Treat her right. She deserves it."

Sutton growled something.

London didn't move her hand until after Stitch had paid for his trinket and left.

They glared at each other.

He opened his mouth and she held up her hand. "Me first. You really thought I'd start up with him again?"

He loomed over her. "You were fucking *hugging* him, London. And it wasn't a bro hug, it was a lingering hug."

"Lingering hug," she repeated. "Wow. I didn't know there was a scale that denoted what kind of hug it was by its length. And double wow that you have somehow memorized that scale."

"I know what I saw," he said stubbornly.

"Then you need fucking glasses."

"Hey, you two get outta here," the woman behind the tables yelled. "You're scaring off my customers."

"Fine." London spun on her boot heel and stormed out of the tent.

Of course Sutton followed. His hand circled her biceps and he turned her back around. "I deserve a goddamn explanation."

"And I deserve a goddamn apology for your lack of faith in me."

He laughed. "Lack of faith? Sweetheart, the only reason we ended up together was to make that man jealous. You succeeded. Every time I've asked you if you'd go back to him if he showed interest again, you've hedged."

"Because it's a stupid question."

"No, it's a legitimate question."

"No, this is a legitimate question. You really think the only reason I'm still with you, four weeks after we made the deal, is because I'm trying to lure Stitch back? Everything we've done and said when no one's been around us was us playing a part? None of it was real?"

"You tell me," he said coolly.

Just like that, London stepped back. "How about when you figure it out you come find me." She stormed away from him.

"How about I'd better find you in my damn corral, working with my horse," he shouted at her.

For the love of God. Seriously? They were shouting at each other like angry teens now?

And she'd never understood the phrase *the devil made me do it*, but at that moment she was so mad that she lost control of rationality. "Don't hold your breath because I'm done with your horse."

"Explain what the hell that means."

"Dial is as trained as he's gonna get."

"And you just decided that right now when you're pissed?"

London shook her head.

"How long have you been keeping that from me?"

"Since the end of the second week."

Shocked, he said, "Why?"

"Because I didn't want to leave you, jackass," she snapped. "I've been in this situation before. After you got what you wanted from me I figured you'd boot my ass out."

"You really think the only reason I wanted you around, four weeks after we made the deal, is because I want you to train my fucking horse?" he shot back.

How dare he throw her words back in her face? "You tell me. If you'd bothered to come out and watch me work Dial, you would've known two weeks ago that I was done. But you stayed away because you never intended to get back on that horse and compete again, did you?"

He bit off, "No," with zero hesitation.

"When were you gonna tell me?"

"When I had some other things squared away in my life."

"Was I one of those things?"

A muscle ticced in his jaw. "Are you gonna let me explain or just jump to conclusions?"

"Like you did with Stitch?"

"This is getting us nowhere. Can we—"

"No. I need to cool down before I say something out of anger that I don't mean."

"London. If we don't do this now—"

"Then we'll do it later." She jabbed her finger at him. "Don't you give me an ultimatum, Sutton Grant."

"I'm not. But please wait."

She didn't. She kept walking until she reached her camper.

Once inside, it was tempting to break into her emergency bottle of tequila.

Instead she breathed slow and deep to stave off her tears. Part of her expected that Sutton would come barreling into her camper, snarl about putting her over his knee to get her attention, but he didn't show.

She held out on checking her phone until after opening ceremonies—but no missed calls or text messages.

In fact, she didn't see him or hear from him that night.

Or the next day and night.

Or the next day.

Since London had a key to his house, she headed there first after the rodeo ended Sunday afternoon. No sign of him. But she could tell he'd been there. She could tell it'd been at least a day since he'd tended to Dial because the headstrong gelding came right up to her. He didn't make her chase him down.

Once she returned inside, she punched in the code and entered his private domain, ready to read him the riot act if he was hiding from her. If Sutton had been in his underground shooting range, she couldn't tell because the place was always spotless. Granted, she hadn't expected Mr. Responsible to suddenly leave firearms lying about, but there wasn't even an empty ammo box in the garbage.

After locking the door, she wandered into the kitchen. But she was too melancholy to fix herself food. Wasn't long before anger replaced her melancholy. The man's avoidance was ridiculous. Did he really think she'd just pack up and leave because she didn't have a conversation on *his* time frame? Did he really believe she'd let this issue stand between them when she was in love with him?

Wrong.

She might be hardheaded but she wasn't a fool.

The man had one more day to come to his senses or she was calling in the big guns.

Chapter Thirteen

Sutton was running late—a rarity for him, so he hoped she didn't give him grief for it. He scanned the tables in the restaurant. When he saw her, he smiled. There'd been a time when his pulse would've quickened, but now that his heart belonged to another, he just had a genuine sense of happiness at seeing her.

He wandered to the back booth where she'd set up camp with a stroller, a car seat, and a diaper bag.

As soon as he loomed over her, she drawled, "Forgive me if I don't get up, but as you can see my hands are full."

"I see that. Will your bruiser of a husband punch me in the face if I kiss your cheek?"

"He's not here right now. He'll be back in a bit, so kiss away, hot stuff."

Sutton kissed Tanna's temple. "I've got you all to myself, Tex-Mex? Well, besides this little guy." He peered at the face peeking out of the blanket. "Handsome papoose you birthed."

Tanna whapped him on the arm. "Papoose. With Fletch's Native American background and my Mexican, August Bruce Fletcher has gorgeous coloring." She sighed and stroked her baby's chubby cheek. "He has gorgeous everything, doncha darlin' boy."

He slid in the booth across from her. "So his full name is August Bruce Fletcher?"

"After his daddy and his grandpa. But we're calling him Gus."

"How old is Gus now?"

"Three months."

"How are you doin' with the new mom thing?"

Tanna's entire face lit up. "Fantastic. I had a rough pregnancy and ended up having a C-section because the kid weighed in at a little over ten pounds, but he's such a good baby. Such a joy in our lives." She looked away from Gus long enough to say, "If you think I'm smitten with our boy, you oughta see his father with him."

Sutton grinned. "I'd give anything to see the big, bad animal Doc baby-talkin'."

She snorted. "Not happening."

The waitress stopped by to refill Tanna's coffee and take Sutton's order. "Just a Coke," he said, "but keep them comin'."

"Wild night?" Tanna asked.

"Nope. Just a long one. Lots of tossing and turning."

"Well, you look good, if that's any consolation. But you always look like you stepped out of a magazine ad trying to sell rugged men's aftershave to men who have no hopes of ever lookin' like you."

"Stop flirting with me Mrs. Fletcher."

Tanna laughed. "Sorry. Habit. So what's up? Not that I wasn't happy to hear from you, but I was surprised."

"I figured you would be. Is it weird I considered it a sign that you'd be in Denver visiting your brother right when I needed to talk to you?"

"Not weird at all." She reached over and squeezed his hand. "I was lost and in an unhappy place three years ago. Thanks to you—and Fletch—I'm now happier than I've ever been. So anything you need from me, name it."

He squeezed her hand back. "I just need the same thing you did—to talk to someone who's been there."

"What's goin' on? Start at the least confusing place for me."

"My accident late last fall? When I came to in the ambulance and I couldn't move, I was scared out of my mind that I was paralyzed. I made a deal with God that if I didn't end up a permanent cripple that I'd never compete in steer wrestling again."

Tanna whistled.

"Obviously I recovered. I've been recovered for a helluva lot longer than anyone knows. My docs gave me the all clear four months ago. My family thinks I'm still on physical restrictions—because that's what I've led them to believe. I've pulled through two bad wrecks and some heavy emotional shit, so yeah, I'm keepin' my heavenly promise. But that's left me in limbo, not knowing what to do with myself if I'm not bulldoggin' for a living."

"I hear ya there." The bundle on her lap squirmed and squeaked and she rocked in the booth. "What else?"

"Dial has been shunted aside since the accident. I figured he'd be okay taking it easy for a couple of months. When the docs gave me medical release, I immediately took him out and tried to put him through his paces."

"How'd that go?"

"Not well. Mostly because my brothers happened to come by and check on me, saw me racing hell bent for leather on my horse, and lost their minds. At that point I coulda told them I'd been medically released and I was fine to resume training. But in the back of my mind? That little voice reminded me training was pointless because I'd promised to give it up and I had no freakin' idea what to do with my life."

"And this tug of war has been goin' on since that day?"

"Yep."

"It's gone beyond you faking a limp and constantly complaining about your sciatica to your family?"

"I see you ain't lost that smartass humor."

"Gotta take my shots when I can." She smirked. "But I'll behave. Go on."

"I hate that Dial became a problem horse because of my lie. I even went so far as to hire London Gradsky to help me get Dial back on track." He didn't want to tell her this next part, but in for a penny, in for a pound. "And I've fallen head over heels in love with the woman."

Tanna stopped moving and didn't start again even when Gus fussed. "Are you shittin' me, Sutton Grant? You and the horse trainer? I thought she hated you for convincing Chuck and Berlin to sell Dial to you."

"She did. But she's a horse woman to the core, Tanna. She trained Dial in the first place. At first she had uh...other reasons for agreeing to help me."

"Should I ask about them other reasons?"

"That's more her deal than mine. But it was a deal I agreed to. Spending all our time together...she's practically livin' with me. She's sexy, sweet, funny, and that girl has a mouth on her that don't quit—evidently that's a trait in a woman that attracts me"—he laughed when Tanna flipped him off—"and damn if I don't like playin' house with her. A lot."

"Does she know you're in love with her?"

Sutton smiled. "Talk about déjà vu."

"What?"

"I asked the same thing of Fletch that day he came to watch you race around barrels at full speed."

"What'd he say?"

"That you couldn't be around him and not know how he felt about you."

Her brown eyes softened. "I was crazy in love with that man then too, but I wouldn't admit it to him either. So the question is, has the tough babe wielding the horsewhip softened up some and is she in love with you?"

"I have no idea. This all happened so damn fast. Who the hell falls in love in a couple of weeks?" Agitated because he didn't do this spilling his guts thing, Sutton let out a slow breath. "Go ahead and laugh."

"Not on your life. But I am gonna play devil's advocate for 'The Saint.'"

He blinked at her. "Okay."

"I have to err on the side that says the horse whisperer—or should I say horse whipper?—is madly in love with you too. How could she not be? You are the real deal, a genuine gentleman and one of the greatest guys I've ever known." She winked. "Even if you are a little shy and reserved for my taste."

"I'da given my left nut to hear you say that to me years ago." He'd been so crazy about Tanna, even when she'd been crazy about Fletch, but he hadn't harbored illusions that they'd ever be together. That just reminded him he had a long history of betting on the wrong horse—when it came to women. Reading more into situations and relationships that weren't there. So he erred on the side of caution. "I just...worry that if London had feelings for me, they'll change like Charlotte's did when she realized I'm no longer interested in living life on the road pursuing another championship."

Tanna angled forward. "You listen to me, Sutton. Charlotte was a star-fucker; she doesn't deserve a thought beyond that. I take it London found out you're putting 'former bulldogger' on upcoming resumes?"

"We had a big damn fight and I didn't even tell her that I knew in the hospital I'd never intended to compete on the circuit professionally again. She asked why I hired her. I saw it in her eyes, she thought everything was lies and manipulation—and she stormed off refusing to discuss it."

"Ever?"

"No. She said she needed to cool down. Then I had to go out of town and everything is just fucked. Been a long couple of days."

Fuck. He needed to get the hell out of here. What made him think this was a good idea? He drained his soda and stood. "Sorry. Wasn't fair to dump all this on you when you've got so much on your plate already."

"Sit your ass down, Sutton. Now."

He sat.

"You came here because you want my advice, not to hear me condone or condemn what you've been doin', right?"

"Right."

She smiled at her baby when he grunted and squeaked. "My precious boy here has changed my life and the way I look at every little thang. So *he* was my promise to God, so to speak. Fletch and I tried for a year to get pregnant. I swore that if we were blessed with a child, I'd slow down. Take a year off from the circuit."

"Are you rethinking that?"

"Right now, I couldn't give a damn if I *ever* compete in barrel racing again. On any level." Tanna looked up at him. "I have four world championships. The number of women who can lay claim to that can be etched on the head of a pin." She bit her lip. "Okay, that ain't true. I still tell tall Texas tales if I can get away with it. The point is, the deals we make with ourselves, the promises we break, all lead to one question: how many championship gold buckles are enough?"

"My brother asked me that same question."

"Did you answer?"

"Nope. Mostly because I was trying to downplay the truth."

"Which is?"

"Even without the injury and the promise I made, I was ready to move on from the road to rodeo glory bein' the only life I had."

Tanna said, "Aha!" loud enough to startle Gus. The baby screwed up his face and wailed. "Sorry my sweet." She brushed her lips across his forehead. After the baby had settled, her gaze met Sutton's. "Once you stop faking your injury, what are your options as far as a career? Ranching with your brothers?"

"They'd let me be part of the operation if I asked."

"But you ain't gonna ask."

"No. I like living close to family and having some acres to spread out on and helping them out in the busy season, but the day to day grind of ranching ain't for me."

She raised a brow. "Still didn't answer the question, bulldogger. What's your college degree in?"

"Business. Not ag business, just an associate's degree in business administration." He sighed. "My dad wanted me to have something to fall back on after I stopped chasin' points and purse."

"And do you?"

He shrugged. "Maybe."

"Don't make me come over there and box your ears to get an answer. Beneath the baby spit up, I'm still a born and bred Texas cowgirl, ready to kick some ass."

"I never doubted that for an instant, Tex-Mex." He took a moment to gather his thoughts. "A buddy of mine is waiting on whether I'll pass the tests that'll clear the way for me to come to work for him at his gun range."

"That's great! See? You've got options."

"First I have to pass my range master certification."

"So? Eli told me you're a deadeye with any kind of weapon."

"It helps when you have a shootin' range in your basement," he said dryly. "Not much else for me to do while I was laying around, lying about going to rehab and stuck in my house. I told myself I was killing time, but—"

"You were preparing for the future," she finished. "So get your shit together, Sutton. Talk to London. Talk to your family. Talk to your friend.

Don't put any of it off any longer."

"She givin' you some of that tough love that you gave her a few years back?" Fletch said.

Sutton jumped. How had he missed the big man approaching them?

Fletch reached down and plucked the baby from Tanna's arms—after he gave his wife a steamy kiss. A long, steamy kiss.

Sutton laughed. "Still marking your territory?"

"Always." He cradled the bundle to his chest. "Hey, little man. You been good for your mama?"

"An angel, like always," Tanna said, smiling at her husband and son.

"I can walk around with him if you guys wanna finish your talk," Fletch offered.

"Nah, man, that's okay," Sutton said, standing up. "Your wife set me straight, which is what I needed."

"You did me a good turn. I'm happy to pay it forward," Tanna said softly.

"Agreed. Anything I can do, just ask," Fletch said. "I owe you, too."

"There is one thing..." He laughed when Fletch groaned. "Since my bulldoggin' days are over, I'll need to find a good fit for Dial. So if you know anyone who's lookin', send 'em my way."

Fletch pinned him with a look. "Chuck and Berlin Gradsky wouldn't buy him back?"

"Doubtful. He'd been a thorn in their side for a few years—before you castrated him—and since he and I were well matched they were happy to get rid of him."

A pause hung in the air. Then, "Sweet Jesus, that's something else that London doesn't know," Tanna said. "That you didn't pressure her folks into selling Dial to you. They wanted to get rid of him."

"Yeah, well, she wouldn't have taken that well since she trained him. It'd be a double blow for her."

"Sutton. You have to tell her that too, when you're telling her everything else."

"It's not my place."

"It is. Does she know you're planning on selling Dial?"

"She does now that she told me Dial has been done training for weeks and the only reason she stayed around was because of me."

"Sounds like she loves you, which means this is fixable," Tanna said, standing to hug him and then give him a quick shove. "So go fix it, dumbass."

Chapter Fourteen

Barn therapy.

That's what she needed.

London pointed her truck toward her parent's place and drove. Half an hour later she was in the shed, slipping on waders, an apron, and gloves. She loaded her tools in the wheelbarrow and started in the stall at the farthest end of the barn.

Two cleaned stalls later, she realized she wasn't alone. She turned toward the gate and rested her arm on the handle of the pitchfork.

Her mom hung over the gate. She smiled. "Barn therapy?"

"Yep. Learned it from the best."

"When you're done slogging through the shit—real and imagined—come on up to the house."

"Will do." London returned to her task. After she finished another stall, she called it quits. She cleaned up in the barn bathroom. Since the barn at Grade A Horse Farms cost on the high side of five million dollars to build, it boasted cool amenities, including a full-size shower in both the women's and men's restrooms.

After London drove the mile between the training facility and the private Gradsky family home, she wasn't surprised to see her mom waiting on the porch.

"Would you like tea?"

"That'd be great, Mom." She flopped on the canopy swing and sighed.

"I'd say I was pleasantly surprised to see you, but I haven't heard from you in a while so I figured you'd visit soon." She handed London her tea in her favorite rainbow swirl and polka dot glass.

"Thanks."

"You're welcome. Thank you for tackling those stalls. They always seem to need more maintenance than the others."

"Some kids do too," London muttered.

"Yes, your brother is always harassing me for legal advice for his toughest cases."

She smiled.

"Talk to me, sweetheart. What's the problem?"

"Sutton Grant is the hottest, sexiest, sweetest, most wonderful guy on the planet."

Her mother sipped her tea. "Doesn't seem like much of a problem to me. So I'll ask how does this affect you?"

"Because he's also the most exasperating. And I'm kinda, sorta thinkin' that I'm half in love with him, maybe a little bit."

"Kinda, sorta, maybe?" she repeated.

London blew out a breath. "Okay. Completely, totally, hat over boot heels in love with that man."

When London kept brooding, her mom said, "London Lenora Gradsky. If you don't start talking right now and give me every detail a mother needs, I will bend you over my knee."

She froze. Hard to believe how much she liked it when Sutton had spanked her. He'd been so...intense. So in tune with what she needed and wanted she hadn't even had to ask. And then afterward, so sweet and loving.

"I'm waiting," her mom singsonged.

Where to start? "After Stitch dumped me for that tiara-wearing terror, everyone thought I was suicidal. I wasn't. Yes, I was pissed, but what kind of freakin' jerk breaks up with the woman he's practically living with via text? Jerks like him. I got tired of the pitying looks and wondered how I'd survive the summer since I'd see them every weekend, and then Sutton showed up at one of my seminars. He hadn't been working Dial at all since he'd gotten out of the hospital after his accident."

"Dear Lord. I bet Sutton was fit to be tied because he's all about that horse."

"He was and I initially told him no way because I hated how he pestered you and Dad to sell him Dial. Part of me was thinking 'what goes around comes around, pal' but another part of me was feeling cocky because he had come to *me* for help." She gulped her tea. "This is where it gets tricky." After she gave the rundown about their "deal," she looked over at her mom.

Berlin Gradsky wore a smile that scared London.

"What?"

"That's my girl."

"You're not...upset?"

"That you used your brains to get revenge and make money and getcha some of that hot man honey?"

"MOTHER!"

"What? Sutton Grant is built, good-looking, thoughtful, and genuine. How could I be upset with you getting with a man like him? In fact, I'm thinking tears of pride and joy are gonna start flooding the table at any moment."

London rolled her eyes.

"Keep going because I suspect we hit the problem part of this talk."

"Yeah. So he insists I move into his guest bedroom. He's all cool and laid back, which bugged me to be honest. I wanted him to want me for real. So I put it aside and worked with Dial. And our first official appearance as a couple was so convincing that behind closed doors..." She sighed. "Sutton hasn't forgotten how to ride entirely."

Her mom lifted her glass for a silent toast.

"The more time I spend with Sutton, the more Stitch and that whole thing just fades away. It seems Sutton and I are headed into real relationship territory, but I feel he's holding something back from me."

"I imagine he's tired of that same old question of when he'll start competing again."

London nodded. "He didn't ask me how the training is going with Dial. Which I took as I wasn't doin' a fast enough job and he feels he can't push me because we're sleeping together. But now...the man admitted he won't be competing again and he's been having me work with his horse so he can get rid of it."

"Oh dear."

She drained her tea and chomped on a piece of ice. "He can't sell Dial. I didn't train his horse for someone else, I trained it for *him*."

Her mother shook her head. "I know you've got an independent streak, sweetheart, but there's where you've stepped over the line. You trained Sutton's horse. Period. Whether he sells it or rides it himself is immaterial. He's paying you for a service." Her eyes narrowed. "He *is* paying you?"

"Of course." Not that she'd cashed the checks.

"There's your answer for that part of the problem."

London locked her gaze to her mother's. "You have no ill feelings toward Sutton at all for him demanding you sell Dial to him three years ago?"

"You somehow got your wires crossed because your father and I don't give in to demands—be they horses', kids', or customers'. We sold Dial to Sutton because they complemented each other. Dial was a nightmare horse, sweetheart. I don't know why you don't remember that. We were over the moon that Sutton wanted to take him off our hands. Sometimes I think your father would've paid Sutton to take him."

London's mouth fell open. "What? But *I* trained him."

"We're aware of that."

"So you're saying the reason Dial is such a nightmare is because of me? Of how I trained him?"

"No." Her mom set the glass on the tray and took London's hands in her own. "You and Sutton were the only two people we'd ever run across who could control that horse. The only two. We even had Dial castrated in an attempt to change his behavior and that changed nothing. We were at a loss. You know how we handle a horse like that."

"You get rid of it."

"Exactly. Sutton offered to buy him and we accepted. We knew you'd take it personally, honey. But we all know that a well-trained horse isn't always a well-behaved horse. That's Dial. When he's on the dirt he's focused, a champion, ready to do what he's been trained to. But the instant his hooves are out of the arena? He's difficult. You would've kept trying to change that behavior to the exclusion of training other horses. We had to get rid of him." She squeezed London's fingers. "I know that situation was the catalyst for you to strike out on your own entirely. Your father and I couldn't be more proud of you."

"While I appreciate that...it is sort of embarrassing that I've been wrong all along."

"About us resenting Sutton Grant? Absolutely. *You* resented him. And I worry you've gotten sucked back into that cycle of trying to fix a horse that has limitations."

She'd never considered any of this and it sent her reeling.

But didn't Sutton ask you that very first day if he couldn't utilize Dial after he'd been retrained, if you'd be willing to help find him a new home?

Yes. But she hadn't believed him. In fact, she'd done exactly what her mother claimed she'd done: she'd set out to prove Sutton wrong.

"Damn. I am a fucking idiot."

"No. You just added the complication of love to an already complicated situation."

"What do I do now?"

"Talk to Sutton. Tell him you know that we happily handed over Dial to his care. Tell him you'll help him find another bulldogger to sell to who can handle a horse who performs well but won't ever acclimate to a normal environment outside the arena." She cocked her head. "What about Stitch?"

"Oh sure, Mom, suggest that Sutton sell a horse with behavioral problems to my *ex-boyfriend*. There's no chance that Sutton would oh, hope the horse would hurt Stitch because he hurt me?"

"Sounds like Sutton is pretty protective of you?"

"Yes. Which is sweet and sorta hot, in a Neanderthal way. Sutton and I had words about a freakin' hug Stitch gave me. That's when it came out he wouldn't be competing anymore. I was mad; he was annoying as fuck. I asked for some time and I'll be damned if he didn't give it to me. It's been four damn days! He's not answering my texts or my calls. I don't know how to fix it."

"He hasn't been to his house?"

"Not when I've been there."

"Does he still have that underground shooting range?"

Again, London was shocked. "You *knew* about that?"

"Of course. It's his pride and joy. He invited your dad over to shoot." A sneaky and slightly evil looking smile spread across her mom's face. "I know one way to get a man back home, and you won't even have to get on your knees."

"MOTHER!"

"What? I mean getting on your knees to beg him. Good lord. You have as dirty a mind as your father. Anyway, call Sutton and leave him a voicemail."

"I've tried that."

"Ah ah ah. But you haven't told him that you feel so bad about what happened between you two, and you know he's upset, so you've decided to do something nice for him to open those lines of communication."

"Like what?"

She paused for effect. "Polish all his guns."

"Oh shit."

"Then tell him you've used a Brillo Pad to shine up the metal parts, but you aren't sure if you should use furniture polish or car wax on the wood parts. I guarantee you'll get his attention."

"Mom. That is brilliant. Twisted, but brilliant." Totally impossible to do with the biometric locks on the vaults, but it'd get her point across. London leapt up and hugged her. "Thanks for listening. But I'll admit you scare me sometimes."

Berlin Gradsky delicately sipped her tea. "I have no idea what you're talking about."

Chapter Fifteen

Shining his gunstocks with furniture polish?

That woman had a warped sense of humor. Seriously fucking warped.

Which was probably why he was seriously fucking in love with her.

Sutton didn't bother pulling into the garage. He parked on the concrete slab and barreled into the house. Shouting wasn't his style, but he found himself doing it anyway. "London Gradsky, you better not have put a single spritz of Lemon Pledge on my shotguns or so help me God I'll—"

"You'll what?" she said from the living room where she was sprawled out on the chaise, drinking a beer.

His eyes narrowed. Hey, wait a second. London was knocking back the special brew he'd brought back from Germany two years ago.

"Still waiting," she said and then took a big swig.

"Where are my guns?"

"Safely locked away in their velvet lined, dehumidified gun cases I presume."

He crossed his arms over his chest. "Then why'd you send me that threatening text?"

"Threatening text? When I said I was gonna help you out by cleaning up your guns? That was me being nice, asshole."

"If that's you bein' nice, darlin', I'd hate to see you when you're bein' nasty."

London leapt to her feet. "You're about to find out."

"Bring it, cowgirl. And bring me that damn beer you stole. I haven't had a taste of it."

She smirked. Then she tipped the bottle up and drained it. She wiped her lips with the back of her hand and belched.

"You are the most annoying fucking woman on the planet."

"So does that mean you missed me?" she asked softly.

Here was the moment of truth. "Yeah. I missed you like a limb."

"Sutton."

"London. I know we need to talk, but c'mere and gimme a kiss 'cause the last few days have sucked without you."

He didn't wait for her to come to him. They met halfway, and he wrapped her in his arms for several long moments, reminding himself of how well they fit together, in so many ways.

"I missed you too, bulldogger."

Sutton twisted his hand in her hair and tipped her head back to get at that sweet, hot mouth of hers. The kiss heated up, and he paused to say, "I like how that beer tastes on you."

"Stop talking and kiss me some more."

He did just that. But as much as he wanted to let the passion between them expand, letting it show her how he felt about her, he needed to say the words. "London," he murmured against her lips.

She flattened her hands on his pecs and pushed, putting distance between them. "Uh-oh. That's your serious voice."

"I have different voices?"

"Yep. There's your *Jesus, woman* tone, which means you're exasperated with me. There's your *Hey, sweet darlin'* rasp that means you're about to strip me naked. Then there's your *C'mon, sweetheart* taunt that means you're teasing me. And there's the softly spoken *London*, which means...I'm never exactly sure what I'm in for with that one." She raised her gaze to his. "So if you do plan to tell me something good that'll make me smile, weep with joy, and throw myself into your big, strong arms, let's get through the bad stuff first." She touched her lips to his. "There's things we both need to get off our chests."

He pressed a kiss onto her forehead. "Sounds fair. Kitchen or living room?"

"Living room. That way if you really piss me off I'm farther away from the knives and you have time to run."

Yep. He so loved this woman.

London held his hand and led him to the sectional couch. After he'd settled himself in the corner, she immediately stretched out on top of him, nestling the side of her face against the center of his chest, pressing her hip between his legs. Being body to body, where he could touch her at will but wasn't staring directly into her eyes as he made his confessions, would make those confessions come easier.

Sutton ran his hand down her arm. "Is this okay for you?"

"It's perfect for me." She kissed his pectoral. "Start when you're ready."

He reflexively tightened his hold on her hip. "You won't take off?"

"Nope. Unless you tell me you're part of some religious sect where they allow you to have as many wives as you want, because I don't share well at all."

"Me neither." He marshaled his thoughts and decided to get the worst over first. "The reason I have no intention of ever competing as a professional steer wrestler again is because I made a deal with God that if I survived the wreck, I'd walk away from the sport for good. I'm keeping my word because in that moment I finally realized how lucky I am." When she didn't laugh or call him an idiot, he told her the story. "So no one knows what really went down. Not my family, not my sponsors, not the CRA."

"How long have you been medically cleared?"

"Four months. My brothers busted me trying to work with Dial right after I'd been released. I chose to perpetuate the lie. No idea why I did. Seemed smart at the time. Then it just steamrolled. But you know better than anyone what happens to a highly trained horse when it's allowed to run amok. Needing your help with Dial was completely sincere."

She traced the edge of his shirt pocket. "I know. I knew when you didn't balk at pretending to be my boyfriend as a stipulation of me helping you that you were desperate."

"Not the word I'd use..."

"After the first time we kissed, I knew I was in big trouble with you."

"Why?"

"Because I didn't give a damn about Stitch anymore."

"But I thought you did and I kept pushing us into bein' more visible as a couple—"

"When all I wanted was alone time with you, my hot man. So you believe me when I say Stitch means nothing to me? That conversation you interrupted—"

"That overly friendly hug," he corrected with a growl.

"Was just a hug between friends. I didn't only ask you to pretend to be my boyfriend to make Stitch jealous. I needed my ego bolstered after being dumped. I never wanted Stitch back. I guess I didn't make that clear."

He sighed. "How did this get so fucked up?"

"Because we both kept following our own agenda. How long did you plan to keep me training Dial?"

"Until you said he was back to normal or that you couldn't get him there." His hand traveled back up her arm and he brushed her hair from her shoulder. "Then I remembered why your folks agreed to sell me Dial in the first place—because you'd keep working with him to the exclusion of every other animal in their stable. So I was selfish, hoping it'd take you a long damn time to retrain him."

"Because...?"

"Because I fell in love with you. I hoped if you had more time with me, you'd fall for me too—when I wasn't second guessing myself that no one really fell in love in a week." He felt her smile against his chest.

London lifted her head and looked at him reverently—and they weren't even naked. That had to mean something, right?

"Talk to me."

She ran her fingertips over the stubble on his cheeks. "I expected you to say you didn't think this was real because you were my rebound man."

"Shit. I should've been worrying about *that* too?"

She laughed. "No." Then she sobered. "Here's the truth. Dial is as good as he's ever gonna get. At least under my training. I've been pretending that he hasn't made much progress because I didn't want to leave you."

He grinned so widely it hurt, then he wondered if he might've pulled a muscle.

"I've been milking this job. But not for money. Every check you wrote me is uncashed. I also suspected you weren't being truthful because you let me be. You weren't gauging Dial's progress. A guy antsy to get back on the dirt would've been out there every day harassing me for faster results."

"You didn't take my hands-off approach as that I trusted you to do the job I'd hired you for?"

"Nope."

"Damn."

"But I'd hoped that you were keeping me around because you were starting to feel things for me since I'd fallen in love with you."

Sutton kissed her then, knowing he'd remember this moment for the rest of their lives.

"So what now?"

"You move in with me."

"Like we're roommates?"

"Fuck no, we won't be roommates. And we ain't playing house either. This is for real."

"I can move my stuff into your room?"

"Woman, half your shit is already in my room—don't think I didn't notice." He held her chin and feathered his thumb over her lips. "Dream come true having a woman like you in my bed every night."

"A woman like me?"

"A hot, feisty, sexy cowgirl who loves me for me. Not because of the championship buckles, the fame, or the money. "

"The money is a nice bonus. But will you be in our bed with me every night? Because that's been another thing we haven't discussed. Your need for space."

"Baby, it's not about me needing space; it's about me needing more time. For the past month I've been haying with my brothers, and keeping you thoroughly fucked to entice you into staying with me forever, and that wears a man out. So the only time I could study for the test I'm taking to become a range master was in the middle of the night. The only other thing that's been constant in my life besides bulldoggin' is my love of guns. My buddy Ramsey owns an indoor/outdoor gun range. The first week you were here he told me one of his range masters is getting deployed for a year. He asked if I'd be interested in taking the test and filling in. Then when the guy returns from deployment, he'll find me a permanent position if I like working there. So that's where I've been the past two days, taking the written test, which wasn't fun at all, and sharpening my skills here and at the range for the firearms qualification portion, which will be the fun part."

"It's a really exciting change and opportunity for you, Sutton! How awesome you get to do another thing that you love to make a living."

That shit-eating grin spread across his face again. She got it. She got him in ways he didn't have to explain. "Thanks. I planned on telling my family after I told you."

"Will you make an official announcement about retirement from the CRA?"

"Most likely. I've been avoiding my PR person, so I'll talk to her about it."

"That leaves just one thing left to deal with." She paused. "Dial."

He brushed her soft cheek with his knuckles. "I asked my buddy who's a veterinarian in Wyoming to keep his ear to the ground for anyone interested in a championship bulldogging horse. Dial needs to work, so I prefer he went to a qualified candidate. Payment, lease, whatever is all secondary to me at this point." He paused. "Why? Do you already have someone in mind?"

"No, but I agree it's better to wait than just shipping Dial off and cutting your losses. As long as folks in the rodeo world know you're serious about finding the right competitor for him, you *will* have interest. Whether it's the right interest? Dial is the best judge."

"I'll defer to my expert horsewoman. But I'll point out you didn't think Dial had the best judgment when he chose me."

"You'll still be harping on that years from now, won't you?"

Sutton liked that London was already imagining a future for them. "Maybe. Unless you agree to keep working Dial until he's found a new home."

"Hell no. He's *your* horse. You can put him through his paces every day.

Besides, I'm officially not your horse trainer any longer."

"Mmm. But you will keep that ridin' crop? Cause I have a feeling you're the type of woman who'll need a whack every once in a while to keep things interesting."

Epilogue

Three months later...

"I can't thank you enough." Stitch kept pumping Sutton's hand as he spoke. "He'll be in good hands. You'll never have to worry he ain't bein' well taken care of."

"That's why we're letting you take him," London said sweetly. Then she laughed. "Well, not *take*, exactly."

Stitch nodded, his gaze zipping to his horse trailer as if he couldn't believe what it held. Then he met Sutton's eyes again. "You're really okay with payments starting in January?"

"This year is a loss for me, at least professionally"—he sent London a wicked smile—"on the personal front, it's been a bang-up year." London melted when he wrapped his arm around her shoulder. "I've no problem waiting until you're starting a new season."

"That's just...awesome, man. Thanks." Stitch smiled at London, his gaze zeroing in on the big sapphire ring on her left hand. "I heard you two got engaged. Congratulations."

"Thank you," London said, sneaking a peek at the ring Sutton had given her just one short week ago. In typical Sutton fashion, his proposal had been a little offbeat; he'd tied the ring at the end of a fancy ribbon and looped it around the barrel of her new shotgun, begging her to make an honest man of him.

"Have you set the date?"

London said, "No" the same time Sutton said, "Soon."

"Good luck." Then Stitch climbed in his rig and drove off.

Sutton kissed her temple. "Whoda thunk, huh? That Dial would take to Stitch and vice versa?"

"Stitch is a good guy."

"Just not the guy for you," Sutton said with a growl.

God, she loved that possessive tone. She loved that the shy man wasn't shy at all about showing her every day, in so many different ways, how much he loved her and how happy she made him.

And she was more than happy to return the favor. To be the woman he could count on to love him through the good times and bad.

He draped his arm over her shoulder. "What's on the agenda tonight?"

"We could pick up and clean the shell casings for the new line of bullet jewelry I've started."

"Pass. I get enough shell casing clean-up duties at my day job. What's my other option?"

"Hanging out in front of the fireplace. Playing cards."

His eyes lit up. "Strip poker?"

"No, you cheat."

"Me?" he said innocently. "I'm 'The Saint,' remember? I don't cheat."

"Ain't no one calling you that anymore, bulldogger."

"Thank God." He pulled her closer and his lips grazed the top of her ear. "To be honest, I don't care what we do just as long as I'm with you."

She sighed. "I'm so crazy in love with you."

"Same goes, sweetheart."

Sign up for the 1001 Dark Nights Newsletter
and be entered to win a Tiffany Key necklace.

There's a contest every month!

Go to http://www.1001darknights.com to subscribe.

As a bonus, all subscribers will receive a free
1001 Dark Nights story on 1/1/15.
The First Night
by Shayla Black, Lexi Blake & M.J. Rose

Turn the page for a full list of the
1001 Dark Nights fabulous novellas...

1001 Dark Nights

FOREVER WICKED
A Wicked Lovers Novella
by Shayla Black

CRIMSON TWILIGHT
A Krewe of Hunters Novella
by Heather Graham

CAPTURED IN SURRENDER
A MacKenzie Family Novella
by Liliana Hart

SILENT BITE: A SCANGUARDS WEDDING
A Scanguards Vampire Novella
by Tina Folsom

DUNGEON GAMES
A Masters and Mercenaries Novella
by Lexi Blake

AZAGOTH
A Demonica Novella
by Larissa Ione

NEED YOU NOW
by Lisa Renee Jones

SHOW ME, BABY
A Masters of the Shadowlands Novella
by Cherise Sinclair

ROPED IN
A Blacktop Cowboys ® Novella
by Lorelei James

TEMPTED BY MIDNIGHT
A Midnight Breed Novella
by Lara Adrian

THE FLAME
by Christopher Rice

CARESS OF DARKNESS
A Phoenix Brotherhood Novella
by Julie Kenner

WICKED WOLF
A Redwood Pack Novella
by Carrie Ann Ryan

Also from Evil Eye Concepts:
TAME ME
A Stark International Novella
by J. Kenner

Acknowledgments from the Author

A big yee-haw! and tip of my hat to the wonderful, marvelous Liz Berry and MJ Rose for asking me to be part of the 1001 Dark Nights project!

When I saw the list of authors who'd signed on, I was…humbled and excited and now I'm thrilled because I can call so many of them my friends ☺ That October weekend was a blast and I can't wait to do it again – although this time I will pull my arm back when Cherise Sinclair assures me the rubber flogger "doesn't hurt that much" and I will be 100% prepared for dinosaur porn readings, jello shots, amazing southern cooking (bacon every day!) field trips, beach walks, wine tours and late nights gab sessions with my roomie Julie Kenner ☺

Extra thanks to Liz Berry who never balked at my crazy texts and just went with it when I made changes to the story/plot/characters…again. This one is for you darlin'…

About Lorelei James

Lorelei James is the *New York Times* and *USA Today* bestselling author of contemporary erotic romances in the Rough Riders, Blacktop Cowboys, and Mastered series. She also writes dark, gritty mysteries under the name Lori Armstrong and her books have won the Shamus Award and the Willa Cather Literary Award. She lives in western South Dakota.

Connect with Lorelei in the following places:

Website: www.loreleijames.com

Facebook: https://www.facebook.com/LoreleiJamesAuthor

Twitter: http://twitter.com/loreleijames

Long Hard Ride
Rough Riders, Book 1
By Lorelei James

One lucky woman is in for the ride of her life with three sexy cowboys...

During summer break, wannabe wild woman Channing Kinkaid is offered the chance to shed her inhibitions and horse around on the road with a real chaps-and-spurs wearing rodeo cowboy.

From the moment Colby McKay—bull rider, saddle bronc buster and calf roper—sets his lust-filled eyes on the sweet and fiery Channing, he knows she's up to the challenge of being his personal buckle bunny. But he also demands that his rodeo traveling partners, Trevor and Edgard are allowed to join in their no-holds-barred sexcapades.

Although Channing secretly longed to be the sole focus of more than one man's passions, all is not as it seems with the sexy trio. Colby's demand for her complete submission behind closed doors tests her willful nature, and his sweet-talking ways burrow into her heart.

Will Colby have to break out the bullropes and piggin' string to convince this headstrong filly that the road to true love doesn't have to be as elusive as that championship belt buckle?

Warning: *This story has tons of explicit sex, graphic language that'd make your mama blush, light bondage, ménage a trois, and—yee-haw!—hot nekkid cowboy man-love*

* * * *

On a drunken dare after too many kamikazes, Channing Kinkaid found herself standing on a shellacked bartop while a bartender named Moose sprayed her chest with ice-cold beer.

"Contestant number four! Strut your stuff, baby!"

Channing thrust out her enormous rack, hardened nipples leading the charge. She completely overshadowed the other contestants. She grinned saucily. It was the first time since her thirteenth birthday she hadn't been ashamed of her large breasts.

Amidst catcalls and wolf whistles she sexed it up, shimmying her hips. Stretching on tiptoe to force the tight T-shirt higher up her flat belly. Widening her stance, she spun on her boot heels, bent over, and grabbed her ankles, jiggling her ass and her boobs.

The crowd of men went absolutely wild.

The tease paid off when Moose announced she'd won the Golden Knockers trophy and one hundred bucks.

"Yee-haw!" she yelled and jumped from the bar.

Never in a million years would anyone she grew up with believe that sweet and quiet Channing would enter a wet T-shirt contest, let alone win first place.

A tiny chorus of Toby Keith's "How Do You Like Me Now?" broke out inside her head and she smirked.

After receiving congratulations from admiring cowboys on the circuit and a few frat brats, she poured a fresh kamikaze in the trophy cup. She toasted herself in the cracked mirror behind the bar and liked what she saw.

She glanced around, half-afraid she'd see Jared storming toward her, intent on spoiling her good time by dragging her off to celebrate her victory in private. The man was seriously antisocial. And dammit, she was having fun for a change.

The Western bar was jam-packed. Jared hated crowds, but he hated leaving her alone in a crowd—especially a group of horny, drunken men. Where could he have gone?

Did she really care?

Sweet, warm breath tickled her ear. "Lookin' for someone, darlin'?"

Channing tilted her head. Colby McKay—king of the rodeo circuit—stared down at her. From far away—he looked a total package. Up close—he was simply stunning. Icy blue eyes, dark chestnut hair and chiseled features that weren't typical rugged cowboy, but rather, brought to mind the image of a brooding poet.

His toned body spoke of his athletic prowess with horses and bulls; his thickly muscled arms and big, callused hands spoke of his skill with ropes. Mmm. Mmm. He was yummy and he knew it. He also was aware he made her skittish as a new colt.

She flipped her hair over her shoulder, a nervous gesture she hoped he'd misread as dismissive. "Hey, Colby. Have you seen Jared?"

"He's on his cell phone over by the bathroom." The eye-catching cowboy flashed his dimples. "Which leaves you unattended. Which is a damn shame. Dance with me."

Her stomach jumped, a reaction she blamed on booze, and not the intensely sexy way Colby studied her.

Okay, that was a total lie. She *always* acted tongue-tied whenever she got within licking distance of Colby, and his equally sexy traveling buddy, Trevor Glanzer.

Jared had kept her sequestered so she hadn't put truth to the rumors Colby and Trevor were the bad boys of the circuit. She knew they were fierce competitors; they worked hard and played hard—on and off the dirt. She'd seen the buckle bunnies of all ages and sizes constantly vying for their attention.

But she, little city-slicker nobody Channing Kinkaid, had captured Colby's interest.

So, for some unknown reason, Trevor and Colby courted her shamelessly at every opportunity. Sometimes separately. Sometimes double-teaming her with hefty doses of good ol' boy charm. It made her wonder what it'd be like to have them double-teaming her in private.

Whoo-ee. With as hard as they rode livestock? They'd probably break the damn bed frame. Or her.

"Come on, Channing," Colby cajoled. "One dance."

Jarred from her fantasy of becoming a Colby/Trevor sandwich, she stammered, "I-I'm all wet. And I smell like beer."

Colby's hot gaze zoomed to her chest. "I ain't complainin'."

"You will be once I'm plastered against you and getting you wet."

He bent to her ear and murmured, "Nuh-uh, shug. I like my women wet. Really wet. I like it when they get that wetness all over me. All over my fingers. All over my face. All over my—"

"Colby McKay!" Flustered by the image of his dark head burrowed between her legs, his mouth shiny-wet with her juices, she attempted to push him away. He didn't budge. The man redefined rock solid. No wonder bulls and broncs had a tough time tossing him off.

"You ain't as indignant as you'd like me to believe, Miz Channing. In fact—" he nipped her earlobe, sending tingles in an electric line directly to her nipples, "—I suspect a firecracker such as yourself prefers dirty talk."

The subtle pine scent of Colby's aftershave and the underlying hint of aroused male soaked into her skin more thoroughly than the beer. A purely sexual shiver worked loose from her head to the pointed toes of her cowgirl boots.

"Come on and dance with me. Let's see if we can't spread that wetness around a little." Without waiting for her compliance, Colby tugged her toward the dance floor.

"The Cowboy Rides Away" by George Strait blasted from the speakers.

The second they were engulfed by the mass of dancers, Colby hauled her flush against his firm body. A big, strapping man, he was hard everywhere—from his brawny chest to his powerfully built thighs. No two-stepping for them. He clasped her right hand in his left, nestling his right palm in the small of her back. That single touch seared her flesh like a red-hot brand.

Lord. And the long hard thing poking her belly sure as shooting wasn't his championship belt buckle.

"You okay?"

Channing nodded, even when her head spun with the idea the hottest cowboy on the circuit had a massive hard-on for her—right here in front of rodeo queens, stock contractors, old-timers and everyone else.

"See? This ain't so bad, is it?"

"No. Actually, it's really nice, Colby." She rested her cheek on his chest and sighed softly.

"Nice? I'll take that, though, I'd prefer naughty." His hold on her tightened. "Be nicer yet if we were naked," he whispered against her temple.

Naked line dancing. That might be interesting. Gave a new definition to the term *swingers*.

Booted feet shuffled and stomped in the sawdust. Men and women whirled in flashes of bright fringe and glittering rhinestones. Finally Colby spoke again. "Can I ask you something, sweetheart?"

"I guess."

"How'd you end up with Jared?"

Because I didn't see you first.

Channing didn't look up; rather she studied the pearl studs on his plaid Western shirt. "We met after he did a bull-riding exhibition. We got to talking and I told him I wanted an adventure. We hooked up and here I am. Why?"

"So you ain't goofy in love with him? Hopin' he'll put a ring on your finger at summer's end?"

"No." Truth be told, she suspected she'd made a mistake in choosing Jared. Beneath his enchanting Australian accent lurked a moody, possessive man with secrets. She had no idea what to do about it. "Why?"

"This don't seem like your thing."

"What? Traveling on the rodeo circuit?"

"Well, that too. But mostly I was talkin' 'bout a classy broad like you shackin' up with that lyin' slimeball."

Channing glanced up. Instead of acting snappy and defensive, she batted her eyelashes and sweetened her tone. "Why, Colby McKay, I didn't realize you cared about my virtue."

"It ain't your virtue I'm concerned about."

"Then what?"

His hungry gaze captured every nuance of her face, ultimately homing in on her mouth. Heat from his eyes raced down her spine, gathering in her core. She felt more exposed than if he'd stripped her buck naked.

"Jesus. Every time I look at you I lose my damn train of thought."

"Why?"

"'Cause you got the sweet face of an innocent and the body of a high-priced whore."

Her mouth dropped open.

Studying her eyes, Colby gave her a devilish smile and lowered his head. Taking advantage of her parted lips, his tongue darted inside her mouth. No hard, fast kiss. Just a fleeting brush of his soft lips. A lingering stroke of his velvety tongue. His heated breath mingled with hers and her pulse quickened. Everywhere.

Oh. As his talented tongue slid along hers, any pretense of her resistance fled. She savored his taste; a spicy tang of beer, Copenhagen and toothpaste. Another shudder ran through her and she moaned softly.

"Does that shock you, darlin'?" he murmured against the corner of her trembling mouth.

Channing forced her traitorous lips away from his lazy assault. "Does it shock me that you classify me as a whore, same as those buckle bunnies following you around? No."

His eyes flashed blue fire, as if she'd somehow insulted him. "I didn't call you a whore. I didn't call you an innocent, either, but I noticed you didn't focus on that portion of my remark."

"Then explain yourself, Mr. McKay."

"I spend way more time thinkin' 'bout you than I should, Miz Channing." Colby didn't miss a dance beat as he smoothly shoved a firm thigh between hers and waltzed her forward.

Also from Lorelei James

Rough Riders Series

LONG HARD RIDE
RODE HARD PUT UP WET
COWGIRL UP AND RIDE
TIED UP, TIED DOWN
ROUGH, RAW AND READY
BRANDED AS TROUBLE
STRONG SILENT TYPE (novella)
SHOULDA BEEN A COWBOY
ALL JACKED UP
RAISING KANE
SLOW RIDE (free short story)
COWGIRLS DON'T CRY
CHASIN' EIGHT
COWBOY CASANOVA
KISSIN' TELL
GONE COUNTRY
SHORT RIDES (anthology)
REDNECK ROMEO
COWBOY TAKE ME AWAY

Blacktop Cowboys Series

CORRALLED
SADDLED AND SPURRED
WRANGLED AND TANGLED
ONE NIGHT RODEO
TURN AND BURN
HILLBILLY ROCKSTAR
ROPED IN (novella)

The Mastered Series

BOUND
UNWOUND
SCHOOLED (novella Dec 2014)
UNRAVELED (March 2015)

Individual Titles

RUNNING WITH THE DEVIL
DIRTY DEEDS
WICKED GARDEN (Three's Company novella)
BALLROOM BLITZ (Two to Tango novella)
MISTRESS CHRISTMAS (Wild West Boys novella)
MISS FIRECRACKER (Wild West Boys novella)
LOST IN YOU (sexy contemporary novella)

On behalf of 1001 Dark Nights,
Liz Berry and M.J. Rose would like to thank ~

Doug Scofield
Steve Berry
Richard Blake
Dan Slater
Asha Hossain
Chris Graham
Kim Guidroz
BookTrib After Dark
Jillian Stein
and Simon Lipskar

Made in the USA
Charleston, SC
23 December 2014